JOKER

RANULFO

KER

JOANNA COTLER BOOKS  AN IMPRINT OF HARPERCOLLINS*PUBLISHERS*

Joker

Copyright © 2006 by Ranulfo Concon

For information address HarperCollins Children's Books, a division of HarperCollins Publishers, 1350 Avenue of the Americas, New York, NY 10019.
www.harperteen.com

Library of Congress Cataloging-in-Publication Data
Ranulfo.
Joker / Ranulfo.— 1st ed.
p. cm.
Summary: A modern retelling of Hamlet, in which seventeen-year-old Matt begins questioning everything he believes in after the death of his best friend and his parents' divorce.
ISBN-10: 0-06-054158-X (trade bdg.) — ISBN-13: 978-0-06-054158-3 (trade bdg.)
ISBN-10: 0-06-054159-8 (lib. bdg.) — ISBN-13: 978-0-06-054159-0 (lib. bdg.)
[1. Divorce—Fiction. 2. Death—Fiction. 3. Family problems—Fiction.
4. Shakespeare, William, 1564–1616 Hamlet—Fiction.] I. Title.
PZ7.R1764Jok 2006   2005017722
[Fic]—dc22

Typography by Dave Caplan
1 2 3 4 5 6 7 8 9 10
❖
First Edition

This project has been funded by the Australian Government through the Australian Council, its art funding and advisory body.

To my ghosts

JOKER

Ah, love, let us be true
To one another! for the world, which seems
To lie before us like a land of dreams,
So various, so beautiful, so new,
Hath really neither joy, nor love, nor light,
Nor certitude, nor peace, nor help for pain;
And we are here as on a darkling plain
Swept with confused alarms of struggle and flight,
Where ignorant armies clash by night.

MATTHEW ARNOLD: "DOVER BEACH"

Two loves I have of comfort and despair

WILLIAM SHAKESPEARE: SONNET 144

ACT 1

GHOST

FALL 2004: A SEASON IN HELL

So here I am in hell. Who would have thought it? Oooh! Aaaah! Ouch! Hell is hot—really, really hot. And there's no cool evening to look forward to. No snows of winter coming around the corner. No jolly spring to frolic in. Just a monotonous room temperature of a million degrees Celsius or Fahrenheit, makes no difference which.

Hey, Elvis, how are ya doin'?

Hey, Hitler! But Hitler does not return my Nazi salute. Thinks I'm poking fun at him. He's sooo serious. Lighten up, dude! But then again, he's already lit up. Ha-ha.

Incredibly, no matter how cremation-hot it gets, the skin does not burn or melt—it just sizzles and crackles, so everybody's still recognizable. It's jam-packed here. Chockablock with politicians, generals, CEOs, celebrities; in fact, I think all of humanity that ever was is here. The joke is God hates humans. He loves dogs, and only dogs go to heaven. So if a child asks you if dogs go to heaven, tell them yes, but you're not because you are a dirty, lying, hypocritical, apathetic, bigoted, self-righteous, self-deluding human.

Oooh! Aaaagh! It's hard to hold a conversation in hell when everybody's screaming in agony all the time. Extreme pain is not conducive to hobnobbing and small talk. Out of my maw: just deep primeval screams, hysterical shrieks, lamentations, beastly grunts, horrendous howls. AWOOOOOOOOOH-HHH!!!!

I hope I get used to it. I have 1,000,000,000,000, 000,000 years of immortality ahead of me. Or until the sun sizzles itself out.

You didn't know that this fine hunk of an orb that greets you in the morn is actually a fiery penal colony. You see, all the stars are places of punishment. So

*don't get romantic when you gaze at the twinkling
stars, for before you are a billion souls crying for
mercy that never, never comes.*

*But that would be nice. To be able to gaze at the
stars, holding hands with someone you love. A soft,
kind breeze. An ice-cold drink. A lingering, mushy
kiss. A river to dip in. Cool, refreshing, clean.*

Oh, if I could only sleep . . .

ME AND MY SHADOW

Just kidding around. Hee-hee. I'm still much alive
on this dumb-ass planet. Except the last bit, which
is true. I can't sleep. Or rather my busy brain can't
shut down—it's just bubbling, festering, exploding,
corroding, spitting, spewing all kinds of thoughts/
emotions/fantasies. But there was a fairy time ago
I could just hit the pillow, bring down the curtains of
my eyelids, and I'd be snoring away in slumberland.

But no more. Not since the birth of Joker.

Who is Joker?

He is crazy, a lunatic, a fool, who laughs at everyone and everything. He is a voice and a shadow. He is inside me. Sometimes he possesses me totally. Sometimes he hides and crouches, ready to pounce. Endlessly, I hear his laughter. He makes me see things—visions, hallucinations, nightmares, epiphanies. I love/hate him.

Before Joker I was serious Matt—athlete, top student, and Mr. Cool of Elsinore High. I had a great mate called Ray, had (actually still have, but the sweetness has soured) a sweet, beautiful girlfriend, Leah—I was one lucky dude. My parents envisioned great things for me. Elsinore, a little Aussie town off the north coast of New South Wales, was of the opinion that I was going to conquer the world. Then it all fell—*crash! kaboom!*—apart on me.

My mum left my dad and remarried.

My best friend Ray got murdered.

Two towers came crashing down—Love and

Security. My soul is ground zero: smoldering ashes and ruins.

At seventeen I have hit rock bottom.

The day Joker was born I was at church with Leah. In his sermon (typically soporific) the priest commented on how much God loved us. Normally I don't dwell too much on what the priest says—I let everything slide by. Priests are Muzak to the soul. But this time a voice whispered to me. A weird, derisive voice. At first I couldn't catch what the voice was telling me. Slowly it became clearer. *"If God loves us, why doesn't He pick up a phone and tell us so? Why doesn't He give us a big hug when we're down? Why doesn't He fly about like Superman and protect people from danger? Why doesn't He speak to us instead of letting anybody who calls himself a believer speak in His name? Why doesn't He make everyone good-looking and sexy? Why couldn't He create a bigger planet to cater to our greed? Why couldn't He give us wings so we wouldn't need to consume oil? Why didn't God create us in His image—a cat?* I felt like I was cracking open my mind for the first time. All my life I had asked the wrong questions. Questions which already had the answers. Questions provided to me by authorities. Questions which did not spit or snarl or scream. But these questions I was hearing were different. They pushed and shoved me out of my comfort zone, led me down a dark terrifying hole, subverting everything I believed in, tearing and churning up my brain. I began to giggle. Perhaps at the priest, who couldn't answer Joker's questions. Perhaps at God, who created us— or did we create Him? Perhaps at myself, who was the biggest idiot of all, who jumped and rolled over when commanded, who got top marks by memorizing and repeating lies dumbly like a parrot. I who thought I knew everything now knew nothing. Big fat zero. Life was just a big joke. I desperately tried to suppress my laughter. Leah kept elbowing and hushing me to quiet down. I couldn't contain myself anymore so I rushed out of the church to let it all out.

I was laughing so hard that my ribs began to hurt

and I thought I was having a heart attack. Sometimes I wish I had died then.

During my hysterics I noticed a teenager breaking into a car and swiping a cell phone, which the owner had foolishly left inside. Customarily I would have done the superhero—Mighty Matt!—deed and nabbed the thief; instead I just enjoyed myself like I was watching *Funniest Home Videos* on TV.

The thief glared at me and said, "What's so funny?"

I smiled at him, like he was my best-ever friend.

"You're nuts," he said.

"I am," said the joker to the thief.

And lo and behold, a voice from heaven said, "This is Joker, with whom I am not pleased."

SUITS OF WOE

SCENE: My smallish bedroom, cluttered, a shambles, like my mind. Desk with computer. Bookshelf full of unloved schoolbooks and loved favorites, e.g. Lautréamont (f***ing brilliant! Check out his novel *Maldoror*), Rimbaud, Nietzsche, Krishnamurti, Henry Miller, D. H. Lawrence—these are the new gods to replace the old creaking God. Unmade bed. Posters of dead rock stars (Morrison, Cobain) and Art Masterpieces, like Munch's *The Scream*. Junk, lots of it, scattered all over.

"There's a pervert hanging around your house."

"Right."

"No kidding, Matt. I've seen him a couple of times. Round after midnight."

That's my friend Bernie on my cell phone.

"Why would a pervert be hanging around my house?"

"Maybe he likes to watch your mum and Claude do the beastly deed." Prurient chuckles follow.

"Shut up, Bernie."

I hang up on him.

My mum and her brand-new hubbie, Claude, have been a pair of pretty randy rabbits since they married.

Night after night I can hear the bouncing bedsprings and lascivious moans. Like a pair of teenagers on a rampage of lust. I find it gross that two adults past their physical prime will even contemplate sex. Like watching cane toads. The beast of two backs. Yech!

My poor dad stares at me from his framed photograph on my desk.

I really can't believe my mum dumped my dad for this monkey, Claude. He is short and stocky; there is nothing noble or handsome about his ever-smiling Luna Park face. Every dinner he grunts and stuffs himself like a foul pig. In comparison, Dad, a former football player, is built not unlike David Beckham in his younger days. When I was a kid, I thought Dad was invincible and that he could beat up Superman or RoboCop if he wanted to. But Dad was a gentle giant, a quiet man who didn't do too much arguing. When he spoke, I listened; everybody listened. I adored him.

Along came Claude, a sales representative of some computer company. He can spin words like a lexicon spider. With his spin he tangled up my mum's heart and poisoned her. He gave her the Barbara Cartland smorgasbord—romance, passion, lust. I expected her to be classier.

THE MUM SHOW

My mum was pure class. I fell in love with her at first sight. She was like a movie actress whom I admired from afar. She spoke very little, but I loved the way she moved, walked (she floated), and smiled (she beamed). She was more angel than human. Me and Dad worshipped her. She was our church.

MATT'S BLOG

LISTENING: *"Poison" by the Gonzago Band*
MOOD: *Mildly suicidal and severely misanthropic*

Dear Cruel World,

Shall I compare thee to a rotten corpse?

Thou art more smelly and more degenerate.

Anyhoot, my friend Bernie reckons a pervert visits my house at midnight. Hee-hee. I am intrigued at who this pervert is. Now, don't you think perverts are funny? The word sounds funny, especially how your lips have to wrap around the word when you say it. It amazes me how many types of perverts there are. My uncle was caught stealing ladies' lingerie from a stranger's backyard. A male teacher at our school was sacked for stripping naked and teaching English Lit. in the nude. (Why not? I say. Poetry for bohemians.) Maybe I should become a pervert. After all, we're all perverts. Our sex-crazed species. (Right now I can hear the bedsprings and my mum moaning along.)

But I want to be original and develop my own fetish. How about those virile garden gnomes? Seek them out in the dark secrecy of the night. Start with my neighbor Mrs. McGornick's garden

*collection. They must get pretty lonesome at night,
lust for some hot human flesh to warm them up. A
gnomephiliac I'll be.*

*But enough with garden gnomes. A pervert I
must catch.*

Signing off,
TheNutPrince

Comments(2):
*Dude, have you ever had sex with a hamburger
with onions in it? It's the best!*

Burgerboy

Catch that pervert and hang him by his gonads.

Vigilantebabe

PERVERT HUNT

At the stroke of midnight I sneak out the back. The
air bites like a mad Chihuahua. I steal my way to

the front lawn. I live in a two-story gleaming white house with big windows that spy on Elsinore. It rises like a castle above the neighboring small houses. My dad was quite a king among peasants.

Aha! I spy with my little eye . . .

A ghost!

My heart starts to thump. Not that I believe in ghosts, but I believe in horror. I know that it lies at the heart of existence. Like my friend Ray getting burnt to death as he lay asleep. Like an earthquake which hits suddenly and wipes out a village. Like a plane crashing into a building crammed with office workers. Horror, just lurking anywhere. Peekaboo!

Then as I come closer I realize it is no ghost.

Nope, just a pervert. Visiting the house of perversion.

Having inherited my dad's tall, sturdy, blond Danish physique, I can handle myself in any fight. The pervert is staring at the house, fixated on it, like he was seeing a vision of a naked Britney Spears. Slowly I creep toward him like a cat to a mouse, waiting to pounce and grab him with my teeth.

Then I recognize him.

"Dad, what are you doing here?"

Dad embraces me, the heavy smell of alcohol on his breath.

"Come inside," I tell him. "You shouldn't be out here."

His voice is slurred. "No, no, I don't belong in there. I'm no longer king of my castle."

"Dad, you're drunk."

"No, I'm not," he says furiously. "I can hold my drink. I can outdrink any man!"

Suddenly he makes a move to run. "I want my wife back! That son of a bitch took everything from me!"

Rubbery legs, he stumbles and falls on his face. Wet grass clippings smear his cheeks. When I kneel beside him, he arms me around the neck and whispers to me, "I'm in hell."

Then he passes out.

A few moments later a car pulls up at my driveway. Bernie scrambles out, excited.

"You've caught yourself a pervert!"

"It's my dad."

"Your dad's a pervert?"

"Shut up, Bernie. Help me carry him to your car."

We lug him—Dad is hefty like a suitcase full of bricks—to the car. We drive to my dad's apartment.

"Bernie, swear that you'll never tell anyone about tonight."

"Your dad's drunk—so what?"

"Bernie, I'm serious. Swear that you won't tell anybody."

He shrugs. "Okay. I swear."

I tuck Dad into his bed. I sit there for a while, but I can't look at him anymore. It feels like a statue of him is being torn down.

Suddenly he wakes up, his face full of hatred and despair. "Get rid of Claude, Matt. Kill him, chop him into pieces—I don't care.

"That bastard was my friend and he stole my wife. I let him into my house. I still remember the first time I found out. He had deliberately made me drink more than I should. I fell asleep on the couch and when I woke up I heard a sound in my bedroom. I couldn't believe what I was hearing . . . it was like poison pouring into my ears . . . so I ran to the bedroom—"

"Dad, don't torture yourself."

"That's when you found out, too. Because I started shouting and you came out and you saw it all, your mum and Claude naked. I wanted to kill him, but you were there . . . you saw it all."

"Dad, I don't want to even think about that anymore."

"Get rid of Claude. Make it like it used to be."

"I can't turn back time, Dad."

"Do this for me. Don't you remember how happy we used to be? Bring it all back. I feel I've been thrown out of paradise but I want to go back."

"I wish I could go back. But we both have to move on—"

"Promise me that you'll try to make it like it was

before. I want to go home to my family."

Like it was before. Love and security stood tall and invincible.

I hesitate, but I know I can't break my father's heart. "I promise."

LIKE IT WAS BEFORE

Excerpt from my ink diary:

September 1, 2001

The first day of spring and azaleas are blossoming all over the little Aussie town of Elsinore.

Last night my family, along with my best friend Ray and new girlfriend Leah (she is hot!), went out to celebrate my school team winning the state football championship (I am captain). We went to the local Danish restaurant Cornelius (which has its own windmill) and I felt so blessed with all my loved ones with me. Dad made a toast to me and the future. Then we got stuck into the Danish food. The gravlaks and Weiner schnitzel were awesome.

I'm one lucky guy. From the bedroom window I can trace the horizon, I see endless blue skies, I feel the presence of God watching over us all, and His Love gives me strength.

Got to go. Mum's calling me down to dinner.

LET ME IN

I stop by Leah's place, tapping on her window.

It takes a few minutes before she responds. She is

sleepy eyed but still a beauty to behold. Her looks are similar to my mum's: blue eyes, brown hair, and a gentle (some say glacial) facial demeanor.

"What's the matter, Matt?" she asks in her soft, delicate voice.

"Let me in," I ask her.

She's quite startled at my appearance, like something a cat dragged in. I look crazy, my clothes muddy and rumpled.

But she doesn't question my reasons and lets me climb inside her room. I need to hold her.

I slither out of my clothes and we burrow under her quilt and cuddle.

"Are you okay?"

"I've just seen a ghost."

"Really?"

"Not a real ghost. My father. Tell me, Leah, do you love me?"

"You know I do."

"Do you love the old Matt or the new Matt?"

"What's the difference?"

"The old Matt was innocent and naïve and caring. The new Matt is angry and cynical and cruel."

"You're still Matt to me."

We fall into silence until she breaks it. "You might think I'm naïve, but when my mother died my father just totally lost it. He drank too much, and at times I didn't recognize him, as if a demon had possessed him. He even hit me once. He was sorry for it later. I wanted to run away. But I knew my mum wanted me to stay and look after him. My dad's all right now. So I know all about men and their demons."

I have a demon and he's called Joker.

And an angel called Leah.

After a while I begin to shake and tremble. I have been having these attacks. Like a ghost in my soul scaring me.

Leah notices it and she kisses me and lies on top of me, covering me as if to protect me.

I have a strange dream. We are on top of a burning building. There's no escape or rescue. So we hold hands and jump.

I wake up with a jolt. I turn to Leah, but a skeleton lies where she was. Then in the shadows I hear somebody. It's a cackling sound. I can't see him, but I know it's Joker.

MATT VS. THE SIXTY-FOOT-TALL WOMAN

The mind is a funny thing. I was so close with Leah last night, and the following morn as I was walking back home I started hating her. I was thinking about how my mum dumped my dad. What had he done to deserve that? He didn't abuse her, cheat on her; he kept his side of the bargain. But she reneged on the contract. How can I predict what Leah will do to me? Do I really know her?

Treachery, thy name is female.

Leah says she loves me. What does that mean? Will she stick by me through thick and thin? I've changed too much. She still belongs to this rotten world and I'm an outsider. Will she still love me when I tell her I've flunked school and applied for unemployment benefits? Will she love me when she finds out her golden boy is scrap metal?

All women want are guys with good looks, big wallets, and small brains. For women are shallow. Leah is going out with me because I'm tall and blond. If I were a three-foot-tall pygmy, would she still love me? As far as my mind is concerned, she despises it. Because my mind is dangerous and unpredictable and she can't control it. She wants the normal life and she won't tolerate my abnormality.

I won't dump Leah. She'll have to dump me. Because I want her to prove to me that love is bullshit.

Joker addresses the judge in court. Beside him on a table lies Exhibit A—Leah's naked corpse. Exhibit B—a pile of magazines. Exhibit C—a television set.

"Your Honor, here is the evidence to prove that women are shallow. They read gossip magazines so they can catch up with what's happening to their

favorite idiot celeb. They watch stupid, vulgar tele-vision shows like Friends *or* Big Brother. *And they don't like Stanley Kubrick's movies. Incredibly they fall asleep in the middle of* 2001: A Space Odyssey *(the best-ever flick). Finally, I would like to perform an autopsy on a female cadaver. As you can see, her brain is made of cotton candy. Her heart is milk chocolate. And her blood is strawberry soda. Sweet the female is, but that's only because of the high sugar content. As we all know, too much sugar is detrimental to one's health and can lead to diabetes, heart disease, and so forth."*

PSYCHO DINNER

Dinner with the queen and the false king.

A hacked lamb roast, fragrant and oily, lies in the middle of the table. A bowl of green and orange vege-tables beside it.

Claude continually grabs more lamb like a ravenous wolf. Mum nibbles and pecks like a dove.

I want to eat and run, retreat into my lair.

But Mum and Claude keep me back with cordial conversation.

Cordial: a) pleasant; b) a sweet, artificial drink.

Mum is so besotted with Claude that she hangs on every word he says. She doesn't notice me anymore. She doesn't even notice that I hardly speak to her. She just doesn't care what she's done to Dad and me. Ripped the family apart. Ripped out my heart.

Claude tries to sales talk his way into being a surrogate father to me, but I won't let him. Vile salesman, begone! Take your greasy charm with you.

Claude shares funny anecdotes about the characters he's met on the road. He titters at his own jokes, with my mum a fawning audience.

As I gaze with contempt at Claude's smug face, I entertain a rather psychotic thought: grab my fork and plunge it into his busy Adam's apple. After all, isn't that what my dad asked me to do? Isn't this the mission? To return everything to what it was like before? The golden days—a time when I believed in love and I believed in the future. Can I accomplish this? Sounds like a mission: impossible.

I slice the lamb and put it into my mouth. I smile at Claude. If someone took a quick photo you would think this was one happy family. But photos don't show people's souls. My soul's dark and dangerous. Not soft and cuddly like the old days.

"Matt," Mum says to me. "I've been talking with Leah's dad."

"You mean Principal Polly."

"Don't call him that. Paul talked to me about your grades. He's concerned . . . Well, I am, too. He wants to discuss matters with you."

I shrug it off. "What's to discuss?"

"This is your last year, and if you're going to university next year— "

"I'm not going to university next year. I've decided to become a politician." I give her a smirk, which is a thing a lot of politicians like to do. I'm practicing.

"I'm sure politicians need a university education."

"No, I don't need a degree in hypocrisy and deception."

"I don't think politics is as simple as that."

"Why not? Love is as simple as that." I glance at my mum, then at Claude. They keep quiet, as they know I'm referring to the time I discovered their lies and deceit. She as a loving wife and mother, and he as my dad's friend. What an act.

Joker in a chef's hat traipses in and plonks a dish in the middle of the dining table. Three burnt hearts, buzzing with flies.

IN WHICH MATT CONTEMPLATES SUICIDE

SCENE: My bedroom; lights off; curtains at the window lightly billowing like white apparitions; I lie in bed, staring into the darkness.

Shall I hang myself or shall I smear my naked

body with barbecue sauce and get eaten by silky terriers? Suicide has been crossing my mind lately. It would solve a lot of things. I won't have to look at Claude anymore and hear his and my mum's bestial grunts at night. I won't have to do crummy homework. I won't have to get a phony job. I won't have to watch our species destroy this planet.

Most important my brain will finally go to sleep. The dead don't have insomnia.

But what happens after I die? So who's right? The Jews, Christians, Muslims, Buddhists, Pagans, Atheists? They can't all be right. Although they can all be wrong. The Muslims got a great sales point with a heavenly harem awaiting the good man. Surprised the Koran didn't catch on with Western males. As for Buddhism, I certainly don't want to get reincarnated. Once around is enough. While the Atheist's Nothingness is too freaky for me. But then the Christian eternal life seems an awfully long time. Some days I'm just too bored to exist.

Who knows the answer is Ray. Bright, sunny Ray. I can't believe that he's gone.

FLASHBACK 70S SCENE*

Me and Ray are hanging out in his pad, listening to vinyl on the turntable. I have long hair, wear a flower shirt, tight denim flares, and platform shoes. Ray is wearing a denim jumpsuit and sports a dark afro and sideburns.

ME: This record sounds groovy. Who's the band?
RAY: Led Zeppelin. I bet they'll be bigger than
   the Beatles. (He hands me the cover of the album
   Houses of the Holy.)
ME (checking out the front and back of the cover):

---

*I wasn't actually around in the 70s, but, hey, I like the funny costumes, silly hair, and the great music.

This Jimmy Page is one super-duper guitarist.
And Robert Plant is one hip cat.

RAY: Hey, do you wanna do something funk-
adelic over the Christmas holidays?

ME (with Godfather voice): You making me an offer
I can't refuse?

RAY: Picture this: Queensland, we surf during
the day and at night we cruise the discos. We'll
meet spunky chicks galore. How about it?

ME (thinking for a sec): Nah. I want to spend time
with Leah.

RAY: You're really hung up on this Leah
chick.

ME: You bet. I'm gaga about her! For Christmas I'd
rather see her pretty face than your ugly mug.

RAY: No worries, mate. You'll be jealous of
my tan when I come back.

I never saw his face again. He didn't deserve to die,
especially the way he did. A sick arsonist started a
fire which burned down the backpackers' hotel he

was in and he was trapped. It was so senseless. His future torn from him. It made me realize that the future is not a birthright. Poor bloke, I miss him so. I should have been there, to look out for him.

But I don't want to join him yet, so I'll postpone the inevitable.

IN WHICH JOKER GETS THE CHUCK

They chuck me off the football team because Joker doesn't want to follow the rules. I passed the ball to my opponent. I ran in circles. I walked on my hands. The clincher: I sat in the middle of the field and read a book.

"It's only a game," I say to my coach as I leave the locker room. Which was like saying to a priest that the Bible is just words. So he gives me a bucketing of insults and curses.

Leah is waiting for me outside, fuming.

"Why did you do it?" she asks me. "You're the most talented player on the team."

"Sports people aren't talented. I consider them lucky that idiots are willing to pay them money to play some stupid game."

"It's not just football," she says. "It's also your schoolwork. Why are you throwing away your future? You act as if you have no talent and no brains. You're not a loser. So why act like one?"

"Don't you like hanging out with losers?" I accuse her. "Harmful to your reputation, is it?"

"I don't care about my reputation. I care about you and what you're doing to yourself."

"I can do whatever I like to myself."

"So I have to watch you ruin your future."

"You don't have to," I challenge her. "You can leave whenever you want."

"I don't want to leave you," she replies. Although there is a pause before she says it. I can detect a chink in her love for me.

"You should go out with someone else, like

Marcello. He's rich, handsome, and wants to become a lawyer. He'll make a great catch."

"I don't want Marcello. I love you!" she blurts out in the end.

I say nothing back.

What would Leah know about love? To her, love is just a romantic movie starring Meg Ryan. She's expecting a happy ending. There's no happy ending with us.

HAPPY HOLLYWOOD ENDING SCRIPT

MATT (looking lovingly into Leah's eyes): You're right, Leah. I've seen the error of my ways. From now on I'll conform and become a model citizen. I'll no longer question authority, for they know what is right for me. I lovey-dovey you, Leah.

LEAH: I lovey-dovey you, Matt.

(They kiss each other passionately, saliva drip-

ping in big gobs. After separating, they burst into song about love and spring and joy and freedom and democracy and globalization . . .)

I notice Leah has tears in her eyes. How I wish Leah would conform to my image of her as a black widow spider. It would be easier for me to stop loving her.

POLLY HAS A CRACKER

Principal Polly greets me in the office. Polly, tagged because his name's Paul and he resembles a parrot with his round eyes with jet-black pupils sitting dead center like an egg's yolk. He is also Leah's dad. Obviously, Polly brought me in because he was concerned about my future, and therefore his daughter's. Now, that's funny how adults are so concerned about the future, while they go about polluting the world, using up all its resources, and creating endless conflict. Really cracks me up—how can one take adults seriously?

He leans back in his high leather chair, clasping his hands like he wants to crush me. His office is dark and solemn; obviously the parrot takes himself oh so seriously. Photographs of his serious, petty life surround the room—him winning some award, him shaking hands with the Prime Minister, etc.

"I know," Polly begins, "that you were very close with Ray. You were as a pair quite inseparable. His death was a great loss to our school. He had an excellent future ahead of him, but this was tragically taken from him. We all grieved over his death. You more than anyone in this school have greater cause to grieve deeper. But life goes on. The spirit must forge ahead. Ray would have wanted you to move to a bright future.

"Matthew, grief takes many forms—anger, hatred, guilt, antisocial and self-destructive behavior. But grief for a victim does not mean that we must become a victim ourselves. I see that your declining grades

34

and misconduct indicate that you are turning yourself into a victim—you don't want to succeed, you don't want to be happy, you don't want to have a future because your friend can't have those. But grief must not continue forever; the healing process must begin. Heal your wounds inside, Matthew. Don't let them fester. Darkness killed your friend. Don't let Darkness kill your soul."

While sitting there I can't stop recalling what Leah told me about his demonic side, the alcoholic who was violent and abusive. Maybe what he says makes sense, but I just can't stop wondering what his demon thinks, probably laughing at his hypocrisy.

MATT THE BEAR

This is my last year at Elsinore High and I've decided to crash. I don't care. If I was a corporation and listed on the stock market, then I would suggest my shareholders ring their brokers and sell, sell, sell. I'm going all the way down. Or better, you can take out a put option and make a fortune out of my crashing. Just listen to what the financial analysts say. "He's a big bear." "He'll get more and more depressed, get into drugs, get dumped by his girlfriend." "He'll flunk school and end up cleaning toilets. He won't be worth more than a penny by the end of the year."

Basically, Joker's given up on the future. My future and the world's. Let me count the ways of our destruction:

a) Asteroid
b) Nuclear annihilation
c) Pollution
d) Disease
e) All of the above
So what's the point of school?
No point at all.

SAY A PRAYER

I visit an old haunt—the church. I remember loving the ambience, the feeling of peace and spirituality. I went there with Leah and felt blessed. I come here wondering if God can exorcise my demon Joker. I'm scared of him. He leaves wreckage in his wake.

I notice Leah is kneeling up front, her fists woven in fervent prayer. I think about going up to her, but I change my mind and sit at the back watching her.

I wonder what she's praying about.

Praying to be rich like a hypocrite Christian?

Praying for World Peace? Fat chance that will ever happen.

Or praying for me. For my lost soul.

Then I suddenly remember Ray. I start talking to God. "Why did you take him away? He was only a kid. It was just a huge waste. He didn't deserve to die. There are so many assholes out there to pick from, yet you pick a good bloke."

I notice I'm getting teary. I miss the guy a lot. But I don't want to cry and miss him, so I leave the church in a hurry. God is a gangster.

"Matt!" I hear Leah calling out to me as I rush down the stone steps.

But I don't want her to see my red eyes, so I scuttle away, pretending I don't hear her.

But she keeps calling me.

Joker screams at her, "Go back to church to your deaf God!"

She catches up with me. "Talk to me, Matt."

I brush off her hand when she tries to touch me.

"Why don't you join a convent?"

"What are you talking about?"

"I just think you'll be happier there. God is the perfect man. He doesn't talk back, he doesn't snore or fart. Why settle for less? He can give you heaven. I can't. No mortal man can."

"You're talking rubbish."

"The world is overpopulated. We don't need any

more babies. No more marriages. Every woman should join a convent and every man the army. Then we can extinct ourselves. Perfect."

"Are you going to talk to me or are you going to rant? I wish you'd stop hiding behind this kind of mask and be Matt."

As if I had unmasked myself, I make a really horrible face and scream at her, "Leah, go away, you are so freaking annoying!"

THE PINK HANKIE

FLASHBACK SCENE: I was a chubby kid at ten dressed up like Richie Rich by Mum. One day while I was walking home from school a pair of bullies started throwing stones at me. One stone struck me in the forehead. A pretty girl with brown pigtails came to me and offered me her hankie, a pretty pink hankie. I was too shy and ashamed to accept, so she wiped the blood off my head. I remember thinking how brave of her to show sympathy to a chubby friendless kid. The girl's name was Leah.

E-LOVE

Swiveling on my chair, I open my computer files on Leah. I have kept copies of my e-mails to her.

TO: Leah
FROM: Matt
SUBJECT: My favorite subject

Leah,
Can't get you out of my mind I want to crawl inside my brain and snuggle with your image lodged permanently within I don't want to stop thinking about you ever when I study I think about

you all the mathematical equations equal you you you when I hit the history books I read of General Leah this President Leah that and most of all I love geography where I can climb and roll and jump and slide and hide in your majestic scenery, your marvelous oceans, your magnificent mountains. So when the exams come I shall get an A on you, my luscious Leah.

Matt, eternal student of Leah

TO: Leah
FROM: Matt
SUBJECT: You are my heaven

Lovely Leah,

I saw an angel and I broke her heart because I told her that she was not as beautiful as you. She said she wanted to take me to heaven but I refused, for I wanted to stay here because heaven is wherever you are. Oh Leah, I burn in loneliness when you are not with me. I can't wait to see you.

Time, fly me quickly to my lover's arms.

Matt

TO: Leah
FROM: Matt
SUBJECT: My night with you

Leah,

You didn't know it, but I slept with you last night. My pillow was your cheek and I caressed it, my mattress was your body and I touched you, and my blanket was your love and kept me warm. Did you sleep with me last night? Did you wake up with me in the morning? Did you receive my kisses I sent by sunbeams?

Matt

After reading through a whole bunch of them I feel sad that I can no longer write those love letters to her. I try to compose a love e-mail to her, but the words do not come, or maybe the angel of love refuses to come. What has happened? Do I still love her? Has my soul become dark, angry, and cynical? Have my days of innocence passed?

Days of innocence when my family was one.

When I dated Leah and we watched Hollywood blockbusters, holding hands, making out between explosions.

When I believed that God sat on a cloud observing us all and loving us all.

When I believed in love.

When I believed in the future.

THE NUT PRINCE AND FLOWER POWER

Noticing Leah's online, I decide to send her an IM. The advantage computers have over reality is the beauty of the backspace. Reality is a headlong plunge.

TheNutPrince says:

>u there, Leah?

Flower Power says:

>(:| just about to sleep. what do u want?

TheNutPrince says:

>i'm sorry about this afternoon.

Flower Power says:

>i don't know u anymore. u r like a Mr. Hyde n
>Dr. Jekyll.

TheNutPrince says:

>i don't want to hurt u anymore.

Flower Power says:

>>:P you've become cruel. there was a time
>u wouldn't even contemplate hurting me.
>but my feelings don't count with u anymore.

TheNutPrince says:

>i'm really funcked up.

Flower Power says:

>funcked?

TheNutPrince says:

>ooops. typo.

Flower Power says:

> funck sounds better.

TheNutPrince says:

> FUNCK!!!

Flower Power says:

> :)

TheNutPrince says:

> so u forgive me?

Flower Power says:

> i'm not letting u off so easily. a girl needs
> more than apologies.

TheNutPrince says:

> i'll send u an e-smoochie. now i press my lips
> against the computer screen n send it 2 u.

Flower Power says:

> i prefer a real kiss.

TheNutPrince says:

> with bacterial exchanges n so on.

Flower Power says:

> reality. messy but i love it. no substitute
> for it.

Reality. Around me my room bursts into flames. I see Ray curled up, asleep in bed. The flames lick and singe his flesh. Joker is dancing in the fire. I close my eyes and start to shake.

LET'S GET NAKED

Joker is crazy. He never wears clothes; he is as naked as a mad gorilla. Streaking in public he shocks all the little old ladies. Priests lock the church doors for fear he will commit sacrilege. From the pulpit he would rant to the parishioners that God is a cannibal and makes stew out of humans. Teachers bar the school gates for fear he will speak the truth. You, he would tell the young ones, are all born to be slaves to serve mammon. Joker snarls and spits at artists and calls them whores. Politicians flee from the mirror he holds up before them. Everybody wants him locked up.

They want him to go away. They don't want to be
bothered with pesky truth.

MOST SEEMING-VIRTUOUS QUEEN

As I stroll through the hallway with a book (D.H.
Lawrence's selected poetry) in my hand I bump into
my mum, coming out of her bedroom. She, wearing
a red kimono–type bathrobe, smiles at me. I smile
back at her. For a second I'm a ten-year-old kid in
love with her. Her smiles were like moonbeams to
me. Then Claude comes out of the bedroom in his
bathrobe. Momentarily he flashes his hideous
nakedness at me. "Gross!" I remark. I slam my bedroom door and hear my mum and Claude giggling.
Then it hits me that the smile she gave me came not
from her seeing me but from what she and Claude
had been doing in the bedroom.

One thing I hate about reality TV shows is their

vulgarity. My mum has become a reality TV show, and I'm trapped in it and I'm desperate to be voted out.

To evict Matt, call 666.

PERTURBED SPIRIT

Later I sneak a peek out my front window and there is Dad again, gawking at the house. The ghost haunting the house he used to live in. I don't want to see him. So I go to bed believing that I can stop thinking about him.

What does Dad want?

Return us all to Eden?

I'm no magician.

I go outside. Dad wants to hug me, but I shove him away. "Get it into your head. Mum doesn't love you anymore."

He tries to punch me, but he's too drunk to hurt

me or even find his target.

Instead, I punch my dad and he falls down. Instantly I regret my action.

I crouch beside him and look at his pathetic face, stripped of all nobility.

"You're not the only one hurting. Mum doesn't love me either. She doesn't even notice I'm around. So we should just both fuck off. She doesn't want our love."

We have nothing to say to each other, for there can be no consolation for our pain. He begins crying like a damn fool.

I understand what I have to do. Move out. This family is over. I'm divorcing the past. My mission to set things right is over. The past is dead and buried, hope and love vaporized. Joker's right, life is just a joke.

I'm falling. Yippeeee! Falling below me is Joker, with a big grin. He shows me how to fall, how to surf the air, how to trip the light fantastic. He rolls over and over, he strikes various poses, he glides and glissades. Awkwardly I try to ape his moves. Joker cackles at my attempts. He is my tourist guide, my puppeteer, my white rabbit, my guru, my nemesis, my remote control, my tango partner, my demented Dante, my nutty professor, my hell's angel on my journey ahead.

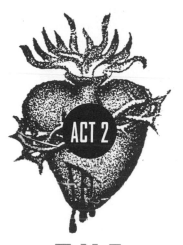

ACT 2

THE UNDISCOVERED COUNTRY

GOOD SHIP *LOLLIPOP*

I sailed on the good ship Lollipop. *I didn't know who the captain was, but I trusted that he or she knew what he or she was doing. I was there to enjoy the cruise, and there was a lot to keep me entertained—casinos; restaurants; clubs; the swimming pool; the whole singing, dancing, bonking caboodle. Then the day Joker was born inside my head like a tumor, I fell into the ocean. I don't remember if I jumped or was thrown overboard. In the vast ocean, waves swept me up, tossed me, and hurled me like a piece of debris. Sharks tried to chomp on my legs. Dolphins frolicked with me. Whales serenaded me. How many times have I nearly drowned?*

The ocean is now my home. To survive I have to

become a stronger swimmer. But there's not a time
I don't miss that luxury liner.

IMPROMPTU

Every school morning I meet Leah at a street corner. Today she's quite surprised, seeing me lug a lot of junk and it ain't schoolbooks. Though she was now accustomed to me springing surprises on her. I don't know why I can't let her go so she can meet some guy and live happily ever after. I ain't Prince Charming anymore. I'm Prince Charles and she's Princess Diana and she has a date with a car called Doom.

"Where are you off to?" she asks me. She braces herself as if I am gonna tell her that I was off to the North Pole and would never see her again.

"I'm moving in with Roscoe and Guildo."

"What about school?"

"I'm done with school."

"You only have less than a year to go."

"Makes no difference. I have no future. I've decided to become a professional loser."

"You're not a loser, Matt."

I put out my hand. "Well, nice knowing you. Have a nice life."

She slaps away my hand. "You're going to break up with me just like that."

I shrug. "You don't want to hang out with losers."

"I want to hang out with you."

"Whatever."

"I'll visit you. You can't get rid of me that easily."

"You really are a masochist."

"And you're a sadist."

"We're made for each other."

She smiles. "Whatever."

She kisses and hugs me. I watch her walk to school. How small and vulnerable she is. If only women were built like men and men like women. That might solve the world's problems. I'm a crazy male on the warpath.

55

It feels great walking away from school. No more chains for me.

"*Go back home!*" Joker admonishes me. "*You are not worthy to follow my footsteps.*"

"*I wanna learn from you.*"

"*You are just a boy—go back to your mummy.*"

"*Make me into a man.*"

"*Sure, but first you gotta have balls, shakey boy!*" He cackles right into my face.

ADAM AND EVE AND MATT

I knock at Roscoe and Guildo's trailer door. Nobody answers. I check my watch and realize it's much too early for them. They have no job to go to, no early train to catch. Nothing else to do, I pitch my tent not too far away. An old tent, a relic from my Boy Scout days. I recall that Roscoe and Guildo were also a couple of Boy Scouts. What mighty men we boyz have become.

The sky is a gigantic blue dome; clouds are parked near the horizon, the waves arguing softly. I sit on the sand and stare at the sparkling blueness. It is so peaceful that one can't escape its meditative effect, lulling my brain, keeping the psycho in me sedated. Above, seagulls wheeling about like feathered ballerinas.

Roscoe and Guildo, the dole dudes, come out as expected at around noon. Called the dole dudes because they dropped out of school a year ago and are living on unemployment benefits. Some unkindly call them the dope dudes, and say it wasn't the sea air they were inhaling that was doing damage to their brains.

"Matthew, what's up?" Roscoe greets me with his big blue eyes and wide black furry sideburns.

"I'm your new neighbor. Pitched a tent beside you."

"Awesome!"

Guildo smiles at me. He is usually silent. He is

one of those who will always look like a twelve-year-old kid, even though he now has some fuzz on his chin.

"Come," says Roscoe, "inside our trailer. We have tea, cookies."

"I'm starving! What about sausages and eggs, something to clog up my arteries?"

Roscoe frowns. "We're vegans, dude. Animals are people too. How would you like it if you were served for breakfast?"

I certainly touched a nerve, so I quickly say, "Cookies fine."

We enter the trailer. It is a thirty-year-old rusty tin can. The interior air isn't too pleasant. On the floor are two single mattresses, surrounded by books, CDs, a portable radio and CD player, and clothes wrestling together.

I'm served a cup of herbal tea and sugar-free oat cookies. My stomach's growling and I'm wondering how I'm going to survive in the wilderness.

"I can't believe," says Roscoe, "that you're here.

That you of all people have walked out of our consumerist society. You were on your way to becoming a CEO."

"An economist, actually."

"Economist! How totally evil!"

"Yes. Now I'm just partially evil."

"You're going to enjoy it here. No stress, no worries, no shopping malls, no ads. This is Eden."

"And you and Guildo are Adam and Eve."

Roscoe laughs loudly while Guildo chuckles quietly.

"And don't you be a Cain, Matt."

"You can chuck me out if I do the Cain."

"Too right."

A DAY ON THE BEACH

My first day of proper bludging. I wake up around noonish, spread myself on the deck chair beside

Roscoe and Guildo and watch the chariot of the sun—the autumn sun isn't hot enough to burn me a tan or fry my brains—slowly ride his way into night. Roscoe and I chat while Guildo keeps quiet. Guildo usually smiles and nods or shakes his head or makes gestures like a mime. He is like a comedian trapped in a silent movie. He makes us laugh.

At night we build ourselves a small fire, the sparks flying and whirling like mosquitoes.

Roscoe delights in talking about conspiracy theories. Somehow the theories make more sense than the stuff I learned from my schoolbooks. There seems a rottenness in the heart of men.

"I was abducted by aliens when I was a kid," Roscoe confesses.

"What for?" I scan the night to make sure there aren't any unexplained lights. I don't feel like being abducted on this pleasant evening.

"Aliens created us humans. You see, they now realized that they had failed, so they are creating a new hybrid. A new improved species. Evolution is another word for alien intervention."

I agree with him that our species needs a lot of improvement. As the night wears on, we feel sleepy and retire to our beds.

Looking back, I think my first day of bludging was quite successful. I've done nothing productive and made no contribution to society. I was utterly useless, and I feel proud of myself. This is what I want. A life without responsibilities or cares. A life without a past and a future. I want to forget about my parents. I don't want to worry about getting a job or an education. A man without a mission. Mission: Aborted.

Joker is a newborn babe. Dust has fallen from his eyes and the world is bright and colorful again. He crawls shakily on the ground and chuckles at everything that moves; he touches and smells and tastes, and all is funny. Joker's smile is so wide, he loves Mummy and Daddy and Leah and toys and kisses and hugs and loving eyes.

Like a newborn babe, I fall asleep, without insomnia, without nightmares.

THE COLOR OF BLUE

Leah visits me over the weekend; I'm really happy to see her. She likes that I'm in an unusual, good mood. Fresh and new, straight out of the wrapping. Mother Nature is a good mother; the sun, the sea, the wind permeating me. We stroll along the white sandy beach, holding hands. She has an orange flower-print dress on. Leah loves flowers. She's a flower herself, resembling and smelling like one.

"How beautiful the sea is," she says, gazing at the blue expanse curling before her. The sun throws diamonds on the crests.

"She's not too bad," I reply.

"I nearly drowned once," she tells me.

"Oh yeah?"

"In my cousin's swimming pool. I was about eight at that time. I remember crouching on the edge and just gazing into this shiny, shimmering blue water. I kept leaning forward as if the water was drawing me toward it. I leaned too far and fell in. I was at the tiled floor looking around thinking that I really belonged here."

"Like a mermaid."

"Yes. I didn't try to float up. I think I tricked myself into believing that I could actually live there. Before I went blue in the face my brother pulled me out, fished me out into the air."

I'm rather amazed at what she said. "You didn't even try to save yourself?"

She shakes her head, gazing into the sea. "Blue is so sad."

"Like your eyes."

"Sometimes I wish I was a fish."

"Don't know if I'd like the scales on you."

I think about Leah crouched at the bottom of the pool, refusing to save herself. I am amazed at such willpower, as if death was a simple matter of switching off, not a frenzy of struggling, fighting. Leah ain't afraid of death. If she ain't afraid of death, she ain't afraid of life. While I'm an unstable atom of negative emotions; I fall apart, go crazy; and how I squeak and gibber, mired in the mud of words. There's a sick part of me that wants to break Leah like she was a beautiful vase. But I know I ain't strong enough to break her. Only she can break herself, and I have this dread that one day she could just walk into that ocean like she was entering a room and close the door behind her and never come back.

THE TIN MAN

Growling monster noises rent the godforsaken hours of the night. It wakes me up in my tent. I go out and see Roscoe, just coming out of his trailer. Out on the beach somebody is tearing up the sand with a four-wheel bike.

"That's Brad," Roscoe points out. "They call him the Tin Man."

"The Tin Man," I echo.

The bike's huge wheels are ripping into the beach, churning what was soft and serene. The noise is loud and threatening like a vicious, hungry animal.

"Because he's into heavy metal and he has no heart."

"Lucky guy."

"Watch him, Matt. He's dangerous. He's afraid of nothing and there's nothing that he wouldn't do. Some people say that he's killed a guy."

"Oh yeah." Funny but the idea strikes me of hiring this guy to kill Claude. I quickly dismiss it. All that's behind me now. I don't need to have psychotic thoughts in this Garden of Eden.

"Guildo fast asleep?" I query.

"He's inside. He's scared of the Tin Man."

"You scared of him?"

"No. But I wouldn't want to get into a fight with him. He'll do anything to win. He'll cut out my balls and hang them as earrings."

As I watch Brad on his quad I slowly recognize him. He is the thief I met outside the church the day Joker arrived. So we meet again. I wonder if Fate has matched us up as dancing partners. I get the feeling this metal freak will take the lead.

I return to my sleeping bag, and all night the bike growls. It's like a lion declaring his kinghood. I envy Brad's outward energy, which contrasts with my inward collapsing entropy. I am a mouse devouring itself, starting from the tail. I am all talk, no action. I'm an inaction hero. I am Super Loser! Super Loser sits on his big fat ass watching crime shows on TV. Super Loser flies through TV channels with his remote control. Super Loser makes food disappear in an instant.

THE CASTLE

On Sunday, Leah and I head off to a multicultural festival, camped on a park next to a highway. We visit the food stalls to get us something to eat. I gorge myself on a kranski with sauerkraut on a roll. Leah nibbles on some Singaporean noodles. To wash it all down we have some milk bubble tea.

We place our butts on a grassy slope and watch the performers on the stage. Doing some kind of war dance, two male Polynesian dancers are wowing the audience with their energetic antics. I feel so phlegmatic and heavy just watching them. After their whirlwind performance, three female Polynesian dancers take the stage and do some kind of hula dance, very graceful and effeminate.

Then enter some Arabian belly dancers, then some Latin musicians. Later, New Zealand Maoris invite some of the males in the audience to do a hakka. Nobody is forthcoming, so they head down to drag some victims to the stage. I'm picked.

Men of various races and sizes line up on the stage. The crowd cheers us on.

The Maoris give us some lessons and instructions. We poke out our tongues as far as they can go. Mine's short and feeble. We yell and stomp our feet, slapping our bodies with our hands. We go through the hakka, the crowd laughing at our expense.

When I get off the stage, I go back to where Leah was. She isn't there. I guess she didn't want to watch me make a fool of myself. I find her watching the pony rides. Excited kids are lifted and put on the saddles of the docile ponies.

"Aren't the ponies beautiful?" remarks Leah.

Something liquid drops on my nose. Looking up, I see that black angry clouds have gathered in great dark knots. Suddenly the heavens break open, and the rain pours down. People scramble for shelter like mice. I scatter off with Leah, not knowing where to go.

Then I notice the inflatable castle has been deserted. Impulsively I hop on, towing Leah with me.

"This castle has no roof!" cries Leah, laughing.

I feel like a kid again and jump up and down, falling, stumbling, and tumbling. Leah jumps too. The hard rain soaks us thoroughly.

We huddle in the corner of the castle.

"How do you like your castle, my princess?"

"Well, it's not much of a defense against our enemies, my golden prince."

"What's the point of a castle if we can't bounce around in it?"

I kiss her wet face. Her skin tastes good.

I want the rain to never stop. Rain to wash away the dust and ashes of my heart.

Up in the torrential sky Joker is paddling a canoe, singing a song:

> *"I'll build a boat of love,*
> *Said Noah to God,*

A boat of happy pairs
On Your ocean of blood."

SPARTACUS: REVOLT OF THE SLAVES

Guildo surprises me one morning when he comes out of the trailer wearing a tie and a crumpled blue suit. Roscoe at tow tells me that Guildo has a job interview. Forced on him by the dole office, which is quite determined to find a job for Guildo.

"It's illegal to be free," says Roscoe angrily. "We all have to be slaves!"

"I don't think you'll have to worry about Guildo getting the job," I say, looking at his Three Stooges tie.

"But why put us through the farce of jumping through the hoops so we can earn our meager check?"

"Well, we're poor and powerless, so they can do

whatever they like with us."

"The corporate world will devour his soul! He's gentle and has no ambition whatsoever in his bones. He's too good for this world."

I watch Guildo amble forlornly down the bush track. St. Guildo walking bravely into the Roman Colosseum, where the lions are waiting.

In the afternoon Guildo returns as an insurance clerk.

THE THEORY OF EVIL

A night of bright swirling van Gogh stars. But no artists to paint them. Just two loafers talking, philosophizing, bullshitting . . .

"The only hope," says Roscoe, "for the world is we all vote for the Greens. Only they will put a stop to us destroying the entire planet."

"I have a theory. It's called the Evil Theory. That

no matter what system we live in, evil will find a way to thrive and prosper in it."

Roscoe frowns at me. "Are you telling me that if the Greens are voted in, they too will become evil?"

"Yep."

"That's horrible!"

"It's true. Look at the Catholic Church, this religion of love and mercy. See how evil people took over and brought the Inquisition and, in the name of God, massacred millions of people around the world. I don't think Jesus had that in mind. It's happened to democracy, socialism, capitalism, whatever."

"I don't want to believe in your theory!"

"It's not a theory, it's human nature. 'Cause it's easier to be evil than to be good. To be good takes time, the soul has to grow to it. Most people are too busy and distracted to nurture their souls."

Roscoe's voice rises in volume. "I don't want to listen to you. It depresses me, it makes me angry. I believe in hope. I believe in the future. You are not going to take that away from me! You know what, I think you're talking about yourself. You've become evil! And you're justifying it with your theory!"

Suddenly the trailer door swings open, and standing there is Guildo, bleary eyed, in his blue striped pajamas, the same type the Bananas in Pyjamas wear.

We stare at him, surprised.

"Excuse me," he tells us. "Can you guys keep it down? I gotta get up early in the morning."

Then he gently shuts the door.

Roscoe and I look at each other, and burst out laughing.

I ponder on what Roscoe said about my becoming evil. I look around and see Joker on the beach, doing flips and cartwheels. He doesn't look evil to me.

TOO MUCH IN THE SUN

SCENE: A fine hot day. The sun is whistling and has his hands in his pockets. Waves gently tumble on the shore. A deserted beach except for two heads sticking out of the sand. Sunscreen lotion whitens their faces like Kabuki actors.

HEAD 1: Matt, we have to save Guildo. The job is killing him.

HEAD 2: Why doesn't he quit?

HEAD 1: I know Guildo. He can't stand up to authority. I've known him since grade school. He was small and shy. I looked after him and protected him from bullies. His dad used to beat him up at home. I took him away. Now I have to take Guildo away from his job.

HEAD 2: Maybe a job will be good for him. He'll make friends, meet girls. Maybe it's you that should be letting him go.

HEAD 1: I don't know. He's not the happy, relaxed Guildo I used to know.

HEAD 2: What can you do anyway?

HEAD 1: What if I blow up the building?

HEAD 2 (shaking): Not a good idea, Roscoe. You might kill some innocent people. And you will go to jail. You wouldn't want to go there.

HEAD 1 (shouting): We gotta do something!

HEAD 2: Leave it to Guildo to do something. He has to take control of his life. He's not a little kid anymore.

HEAD 1: Poor Guildo. A nine to five for the next fifty years. I can't stand the thought!

(The two heads close their eyes and sink back to sleep.)

GOD'S BODKIN

Joker is now king of the beach.

Joker borrows Guildo's telescope and, standing knee-deep in the shallow surf, points it at the horizon. Just endless blue sea, waves ceaselessly crashing. He pans about, hoping for some exciting vista. He comes upon an old Vietnamese man sitting on the porch of his home watching the people walk by.

Joker closes up on his face; it is calm and curious. He catches Joker looking at him and waves hello. Pointing the telescope in another direction Joker sees children playing. Like typical children they are running and shouting and laughing. Joker can't tell which country they are in. Then a bomb explodes among them. Joker points his telescope in another direction. But only more bloodshed. Soldiers are shooting. Tanks are firing. They are trying to conquer a hill, but it is well defended. There are casualties galore. Then he shifts away and sees squalid ghettos swarming with thin, undernourished people. A dirty brown river flows by, children bathing in it and drinking from it. Joker turns to the north and there is an Eskimo beside his igloo; his face is anxious, for his igloo is melting from the hotter climate. Joker makes a 180-degree turn toward Elsinore, and he focuses on Leah in her bedroom. He pruriently wants to see her naked. Instead he finds her lying in bed and it appears that she's crying. Then raising the telescope toward the clouds, he makes out angels.

They appear bored and listless. Some are drinking wine from bottles. One angel vomits, bits of which spatter the lens of Joker's telescope. Joker moves the telescope away and is startled to see a giant eye staring back. It belongs to God.

With His large hairy hand God grabs and picks up Joker and pops him in His mouth to eat him. He smiles, for Joker tastes sweet, then He grimaces, for in the center Joker is bitter. He spits him out and Joker falls on the beach, chewed up and bloody.

Joker laughs and cries and laughs and cries.

THE WAVES

Roscoe bursts frantically from the beach as if he has seen a ghastly specter. "You have to see this!"

I stand up and discern a white figure on the beach. "What's that?" I think of my father the ghost. Has he come here to recall me to my mission?

Dare I return to Elsinore?

Guildo skedaddles into the trailer, frightened.

Roscoe and I approach the apparition cautiously. But it's no ghost. Simply a man in a white costume, raising his hand to stop something.

"Stop! Cease!"

He turns to us. His face is ghastly white; his lips are large and red; his eyes, crying black mascara. It quickly dawns on us that he belongs to the clown species. Big round blue buttons file down the middle of his muddy white suit. A large lace ruffle cradles his head. His elongated shoes, soaked and sandy.

"What's up, man?" asks Roscoe.

"I'm demanding the waves cease their malicious chattering."

The clown is clearly drunk, his eyes glazed and cracked.

"But they don't listen to me. Don't they know who I am? I'm Osric the clown! Australia's greatest clown!"

He darts to the water's edge, lashing out at the

low, tumbling surf. "Take that! I'll bruise you for your impudence!"

He charges forward, getting waist deep, punching the incoming crests of waves. Deeper and deeper he goes, thrashing his fists. Fearing for his life, we run into the angry waves and drag him back to shore.

"Osric," a voice cries out. It came from a midget, wearing an impresario suit. I'm beginning to wonder if aliens from the Clown Planet are invading us.

"Osric, get away from the water. You'll drown."

"No fear of that. The sea despises me. It will never have me."

The midget grabs Osric's arm and leads him away from the water's edge. Osric collapses in a drunken stupor.

"Poor Osric."

"What's the matter with him?"

"Theresa the bearded lady left him for Hercules."

"Hercules. I suppose he's the strongest man on earth."

"Do you know him?"

"I took a stab. What are you guys doing here?"

"The circus is in town. I don't think Osric's fit to perform. He's utterly heartbroken."

Then a tall muscly man appears, striding toward us. I assume he is Hercules. Trailing behind him—a bearded lady. Theresa, I presume.

"Hercules, carry him back to the circus, will you?" the midget asks him.

Nodding, Hercules hauls the clown heap over his shoulders and trudges forward without saying a word. I guess the bearded lady likes the strong silent type. The midget and Theresa follow him, hopping on his incredibly large footprints.

JOKER THE CLOWN

Joker, playing a flute, leads a merry band of children of all races and religions. He travels from town to town, picking up more children to follow him.

Finally he takes them all inside a luridly colored restaurant, where they queue up to buy hamburgers. He goes to his office behind the counter and laughs at all the money piled up on his desk. He tosses it up in the air and lets it all rain on him. He does a little jig, lifting his hands up in celebration.

He goes to the bathroom and catches a reflection of himself in a mirror. A ridiculous-looking man wearing a ridiculous outfit. He hisses at the image, balling his fists.

THE STRANGER

A stranger appears in the morning, as Roscoe and I are laid out on our sundeck chairs.

"I'd like to thank you for making sure I didn't drown last night."

We frown, wondering who this nut is. Then it hits us. "You're Osric the clown!"

He certainly looks different. As a clown he seemed invincible. Now his naked face is weary and sad.

"Ex-clown."

"You quit?"

"Yeah. I can't be funny anymore."

"Because of Theresa?"

"Not just her. I've been thinking about quitting for a while. I just felt I wasn't doing something to make the world a better place. If you haven't noticed, the world needs a lot of fixing."

"So what are you going to do?"

He stares at the waves. "I don't know yet. I want to become politically active."

"What we need is someone to save the world from politicians," says Roscoe.

"Too true. You know what it means to be political? It means to think, to be informed, to protest, to vote. Well, I want to change all that. I'm going out to spread the news. Remember how Christianity began. It began with one man, then twelve apostles went out and preached and in time they conquered half the world. And they didn't even have the Internet back then."

We wish him luck. Lots of it.

"As appreciation of what you did last night I'm bestowing on you my clown gear." A large sack is dumped on our feet.

"Hey, do you think there's a clown vacancy at the circus?" Roscoe asks him.

"I guess there is."

"My friend Guildo needs a job. His office job is killing his soul. I think he'll make a great clown."

"He's a natural." I give my endorsement.

"Can he make sad children smile?"

"I'm sure he can," answers Roscoe.

ON FORTUNE'S CAP

That night Guildo receives the news excitedly. It's as if he is being busted from prison. He quickly tries on the costume. It fits him to a tee. He does a few cartwheels. Looking at him I know he was born a clown. Osric helps him put some makeup on.

"Guildo," Osric says to him, "you are now a clown. What you must understand about clowns is that you can't take yourself or the world seriously. Life is just a joke. You wear this mask not to hide your real self. In fact the paradox of a clown's mask is to show his real self. That he is a fool and nothing else. From now on nobody will take you seriously."

We trek a couple of miles to the circus to get a job for Guildo. The interview is quick and snappy. Guildo is hired as an apprentice clown. They also find a job for Roscoe as a lion tamer's apprentice. Although the lazy old lions don't seem to need much training—they're more like large pussy cats.

FISHMONGER

I feel somehow betrayed by Roscoe and Guildo. I thought we three could have a beach kingdom, subject to no laws but our own whims. But now I am alone in my paradise. I see Joker in the sea waving at me. I wade into the water and begin to swim. A strong swimmer, I make great strides. I look back and see the beach is just a thin strip. I wonder how far I can swim. Maybe I can reach an island. Maybe a shark will gobble me up. Maybe like Jonah a whale will swallow me up. But I can't stop hearing from the waves the whisper of my father to resume my mission—to make it all good again. I argue with him that it is beyond me, I don't have it within me to perform miracles, that I can't rebuild what has disintegrated into dust. How can I save him when I can't save myself?

I let myself sink. I will become one with the

ocean. No more Matt, just plankton to be gobbled up by little fishes. "Is that all you really are?" I hear Leah's voice speak to me. I look above and I see a shimmering light. My angel Leah, still trying to save me. I laugh. Instantly I remember the laughs Leah and I had. We had fun, I can't deny that. As I sink deeper, the light gets farther away. I peer down into the impenetrable deep, and I am to disappear into all that vast emptiness. Is this all I am? What about my hopes, my dreams, my desires—will they sink and dissolve with me? I force myself to struggle. I know I can't give up. I want to be Matt and be what he can be. Matt the man. I want to think, love, hate, fuck, shit, piss, create, destroy, sing, dance. I'm not plankton, I'm a living, breathing, thinking human. I begin my swim back to shore.

I want to celebrate my humanity. What better way than to have a party.

I send out invitations to my beach party to end all beach parties.

ROSCOE, GUILDO, AND MATT
INVITE YOU TO OUR LUAU.

NEXT SATURDAY NITE

COME IN HAWAIIAN SHIRTS OR HULA SKIRTS
OR ITTY-BITTY YELLOW BIKINIS.

PUNCH AND FINGER FOOD WILL BE SERVED.

A NITE OF PAGAN FESTIVITIES.

Roscoe, Guildo, and I motor downtown to pick up some party supplies. The ex-dole dudes go to Vinnie's to get some Hawaiian shirts. They come out of the shop un-Hawaiian. Instead, Roscoe is wearing a scuba outfit, while Guildo does a Harpo imitation, in bright yellow curly wig, trench coat, and squeeze horn.

"We're not having a costume party," I tell them.

"I've always wanted to explore the deep

unknown," Roscoe explains.

"And what's with Harpo?"

Honk honk is Guildo's reply.

"Matt," says Roscoe, "get spontaneous."

Honk.

"I suppose one honk means yes?"

Honk.

"You're an idiot, Guildo," I tell him.

Honk honk.

"Two honks mean no?"

Honk.

"Hey, Matt," says Roscoe, "are there going to be a lot of babes?"

"What's a beach party without girls?"

"Um . . . a gay party? Is that the answer?"

I roll my eyes.

We file into the car. I glance at Roscoe's feet on the pedals. "You're not going to drive in those flippers?"

"I sure am." He grins and starts up the engine.

Honk.

"Will you shut up, Guildo."
Honk honk.

BEACH PARTY

It is still light when the first guests arrive. Piles of wood are ready to be lit for our bonfire. The weather's pleasant and the clouds are like lambs browsing on the blue grass.

The Beach Boys start singing their harmonies from the CD speakers. It's time to party! Leah arrives in a bikini top and hula skirt. She shines and glows. Roscoe lights the bonfire. It begins weak and tentative, but it grows meaner and hungrier. It demands sacrificial virgins and babies. Sorry, there aren't any available, so it has to settle for wood, twigs, and marshmallows.

I dance the Watusi with Leah, who dances with her usual reserve. I loosen my limbs, not caring how foolish I look. Tonight we are savages that worship the fire and the moon and the stars and the ocean. Civilization is a distant memory.

I notice among the lurid Hawaiian shirts a black-clad figure who doesn't belong here. It's the Tin Man. A gate-crasher, and I wonder if he's looking for trouble. His eyes are hard like a lion's, watching out for available prey. He checks me out, smiles, and raises a can of beer.

I mosey up to him. "My name's Matt." Shake his hand, which is powerful. I look at his eyes, which are very intense and the blackest of black.

"My name's Brad. Can I join your party?"

"Not a problem. As long as you leave all excess testosterone at the door. It's a fun, happy party."

"Sure." He casts his eyes on Leah, and smiles shyly at her.

I introduce Leah to him.

"Hi," he says.

"You know Matt?" she asks.

"Yes, we met at church." He gives me the knowing look.

"I don't remember you there," Leah says.

"I have too many sins, so I stay outside."

Leah doesn't want to get friendly, so she discontinues the conversation.

Brad smiles at Leah, and then walks away.

"He scares me," remarks Leah.

"I think he likes you."

"Is that an elephant?" gasps Leah.

I look where her gaze is directed. Indeed, there is an elephant plodding on the sand. An elephant wearing a giant billowing Hawaiian shirt. Accompanying him are members of the circus, all in beach party gear. This is going to be one great party. Weird, but great.

Guildo scrambles to greet them. Roscoe in his diving gear is slower to follow. Everyone at the party goes over to check them out.

I hail them. "Welcome to the party. You are our

special guests. We are envious of your talent. You are all artists. The circus is the holiest of all churches and the truest of all truths. Please enjoy our hospitality. Imbibe and engorge to your hearts' content."

A LITTLE PATCH OF GROUND

The party is in full swing. We are all rocking like savages. Even the elephant is dancing, swaying side to side. Everyone's happy.

I'd expected Brad to misbehave, picking a fight or two. But, strangely, he behaves and is friendly toward everyone. I sense that he fancies Leah and that is the reason he is acting civilized.

Leah is enjoying herself with me. I'm glad; it seems like the old days.

Then I notice some guys whom I don't recognize. They didn't go to our school. Drunk, they start hitting on the girls, who are with their boy-friends. Arguments erupt.

I head toward them, fearing that a scuffle will break out.

However, Brad approaches the strangers and speaks to them quietly. They reluctantly begin leaving, following Brad.

MORE THINGS ON HEAVEN AND EARTH

The party is subsiding, guests are departing, and some have fallen asleep or unconscious here and there. The fire has dwindled into glowing embers. I sit on the beach with Leah asleep on my lap, the waves churning, churning. It's like a giant washing machine, cleaning my soul, wringing the filth, the stains, and the darkness out of it. I am a fresh, clean shirt ready to impress the world.

Then I see a teenager emerge from the waves.

Slowly I recognize him—Ray! I gently extricate myself from Leah and stagger tipsily to him.

"You're dead," I gasp to him.

"Thanks for reminding me."

We then hug each other.

"So how are things?" I ask him.

"Not too bad for a guy who got burnt to death."

"What was that like? Did it hurt?"

"It's like having a baby, except you're being born to a new world. The pain was intense, but the peace that came after was far more intense."

"I miss you, man."

Leah stands beside me, puzzled. "Who are you talking to?"

"Ray."

"There's nobody here."

Ray chuckles. "She thinks you're cuckoo."

"Can't you see him, Leah?"

"I better leave you two lovebirds," says Ray.

"Don't go. We've got heaps to talk about."

"No, can't stay. I'm just here to tell you that I'm

all right. Plus, be happy. Look after Leah, she really loves you."

Ray then starts wading back into the waves.

"Hey, will I see you again?" I ask him.

"Depends on the choices you make."

The choices I make . . .

I watch the waves gulp him down.

"See you, mate."

"You've drunk too much, Matt."

I embrace Leah. "I'm so glad that you're here."

I'm glad that she'll be with me when I get back to Elsinore. I'll need her strength. I feel like a toddler learning to walk.

ACT 3

THE PLAY'S
THE THING

THE PRODIGAL SON

"Hi, Mum."

"Hi, Matt."

We say nothing for a while, looking at each other, feeling slightly embarrassed like strangers.

"Are you back for good?" she asks me, smiling.

I feel annoyed. I've expected, I suppose, a prodigal son's return and being greeted with celebration. Instead, I feel I've intruded into her private home, her honeymoon with Claude.

I enter my room. I had the freedom of the beach, and now I must slink into my hole. I have returned as a mouse.

DAYDREAM BELIEVER

I wake up to the beautiful face of my mother, sitting beside me on the bed, her white, elegant hands stroking my hair. She greets me with her radiant smile.

"Are you still mad at me?"

I don't answer her.

"You know I can't bear the thought of you hating me. You know I love you so much, Matt."

"Do you?" I ask her, testing her.

"Yes, I'll do anything for you. You know that. I'll do anything for you."

"Will you leave Claude and go back to Dad for me?"

"If that's what you want."

"Yes."

I check the clock and realize it is near time to get ready for school. No more time to daydream about my mother. It was a good daydream, though.

THE BOX

Back at school. Back inside the box. After ten minutes I miss the beach already. O for the music of the waves. My concentration is shot to pieces. I can't listen to what the teacher is saying. I'm bored. As I pan around me, I observe that my classmates are just as bored as me. Some are doodling in their notebooks; some daydreaming; some quietly chatting with their neighbors.

But I must persevere. This is the real world. The world of boxes.

I ponder about my future since I've decided to have a future. Now I gotta figure out what to do. I don't know if I can work in a box for the rest of my life. But at the same time I know physical work is not for me either. I want to think, to philosophize, and to be free to do whatever I please. There aren't too many jobs like that. How I hate this world of boxes. I wish people were more laid-back, easygoing, more philosophical. But the world has turned into a giant Olympic Games, and everybody has to scuttle faster and faster and smash more and more records. Slowing down is not an option. We have to be faster than time. Enough already!

Be slow. Go slow. Slow down. Take it easy. I'm a snail. I'm a turtle. Relax. Take an hour off to contemplate a flower. Less is better. Small is fine. I don't want any fries, thanks. There's enough for everybody. War is stupid, communication is smarter. I'm a slug for peace. Wars should be fought with paint bombs. Politicians should wear clown suits. I am the grass. I am the sky. Silence. *Zzzz . . .*

"Wake up, Matt."

I open my eyes. My teacher is glaring at me.

Joker jumps up and dances and sings. The students throw things at him, but he persists. Joker picks up an electric guitar and he strums, and out comes the most loudest, scariest, beautifulest sounds ever. He struts and bounds and leaps, and the students stand up and go crazy, cheering and stamping their feet.

"I'm going to be an artist," I blurt out to my teacher.

"Thanks for sharing that with us, Matt," he replies sarcastically.

The whole class snickers and laughs at me.

I don't care. I'm a man with a mission: Art!

ROCK-AND-ROLL NOVELIST

Leah's involved in Student Theater. I came along to watch them prepare for a production of *South Pacific*. Leah played Liat, a mute Asian beauty courted by the American lieutenant Cable. I enjoyed the performance. It moved me. I can't deny I had my hankies out. I want to be part of this. Maybe the world of theater is the box for me. But neither can I act or sing. What can I do? I thought perhaps I'd write a play. That's it. I'm going to be a writer. I shall rage, lament, expose, lacerate, explode, beautify, excoriate. I'm going to write like I'm riffing a guitar. My books will be loud and will come with an electric plug. A rock-and-roll novelist!

I have a word with the director, a classmate of mine, and tell him that I'm going to write a play. He eyes me like I am a deluded fool. I ask him if he'll stage the play for me. He laughs at me. So be it. I shall form my own theatrical troupe. I shall gather my actors from the dregs of our school—the geeks, the outsiders, the losers, and the lepers. I shall name it the Theater of Truth. It will be my dagger against lies.

MATT CHRIST

Like Jesus, I set out to seek my twelve apostles. Twelve actors for my Theater of Truth. Twelve messengers. During recess I scan the faces of students. I want dregs. Give me dregs!

The first I pick is, appropriately, called Peter. Friendless, face cratered with living and dead acne, breath that could kill a flower. He speaks softly, not having had a conversation for a long while.

Then Sharon, teased by her classmates for her close resemblance to Little Lotta, the famous obese cartoon girl.

George—a Greek stamp collector. Daily brings his stamp album hoping to show it one day to someone who might be interested. Nobody cares a fig. He glows with joy as I browse his stamps.

Phuong—Vietnamese girl who hates her parents because they want her to be a doctor. She wants to be a waitress.

Steve—has severely low self-esteem. His father is cynical, his mother sarcastic. They use him for target practice.

Lara—lonely lesbian. Writes poetry about dead pets.

Deano—vandal, firebug. Lost all his teeth in a fight.

Nongnong—Thai, teased for his name. Otherwise, handsome and has a beautiful singing voice.

Oswald—pompous, pedantic. Likes to wear bow ties.

Changi—comedian wannabe. Nobody laughs at his jokes. I tell him his jokes are posthumous: only a future generation can understand and appreciate his humor. This brightens him up.

Stella and Shana—Siamese twins. They have no friends, and they hate each other.

Behold my Theater of Truth. We shall triumph over the world of lies. Within and without. Lies of lovers, lies of politicians. I am rotten, therefore the world is rotten. This tiny seed will grow into a mighty tree, roots delving into the earth's core, branches to form a canopy in the sky. The virus has been unleashed on an unsuspecting world . . .

GRAVEYARD JINKS

In my bedroom I set out to write my play. This should be easy. I stare at the virgin page for hours. I maraud the fridge for carbo to fuel me. Still the page remains a virgin intact. I despair at my deficiency of talent. Then I laugh at my delusions of grandeur. Theater of Truth. Ha ha-ha-ha. Theater of idiots, more likely!

Picking up my economics book, I begin studying the theories and formulations. Oh well, perhaps I can become an economist and wipe out poverty. After a few minutes, I start chuckling, then giggling, laughing until I burst out into full-out guffawing. The book has obviously been written by a madman. What have all these numbers to do with sick and dying children? I throw this sickening tome at the wall.

I stand up and press my forehead against the

window. Dark outside, reflecting my inside. A motorbike pulls into my driveway. The Tin Man. He sees my silhouette at the window and motions me to come down. Desperate to get out of my room, I trot down the stairs.

"What's up?" I ask him.

"Wanna ride the whirlwind?"

"Okay."

I straddle the bike behind him and hold him around his waist. He throttles forward and we fly down the road. He gathers speed and we race through the dark and empty streets of Elsinore. I feel safe somehow. Brad is in total control. I envy him in that. That he's strong and he doesn't wallow in words and feelings like I do—where between thought and action lie a hundred mental reactions.

We enter a bar called Ophelia.

I drink to drown my artistic impotence.

"You ever killed a guy?" I ask Brad after a couple of beers.

"Why you ask?"

"I once thought about killing somebody."

"Yeah. Who?"

"Claude. My stepfather."

He takes a long look at me, sizing me up, and sniggers.

"You're no killer. You'll never be."

"Why not? After all, if I were a soldier and sent to battle I'm sure I could pull the trigger."

"That's different. It's kill or be killed in a battle-field. You have no choice. But you have a choice."

"And you think I'll choose not to kill."

"Sure. Because you've got a lot to lose and got nothing to gain. You'll lose Leah. Freedom. While for me, I could kill 'cause I ain't got nothing to lose."

"What about your freedom?"

"The world is a prison to me, mate."

I wonder why Brad likes me. Because he likes Leah? Maybe we can help each other. I'll teach him about being civilized, and he'll teach me about being barbaric. I'll teach him how to lie, cheat, and climb the ladder of success (he can have my economics book). While he'll teach me how to kill Claude.

IN WHICH JOKER FINDS INSPIRATION

Joker is prostrate on the front lawn, staring at the endless black void. He is moaning and groaning in self-pity. He can feel himself falling straight into it. Then he notices the stars that net the darkness. The stars, globules of light, that will save him from falling. Holding up his arms to the stars, he can feel them sending their powerful energy into him, igniting brain cells. Light of the universe, light of creation, God, Zeus, Buddha, Stanley Kubrick—Eternal Artist. He is inspired, ready to write. He sprints home to get to pen and paper. His pen is his sword to cut, thrust, slice, carve, chop, hack, and murder. And the ink is

blood, blood of his enemies—lies, hypocrisy, illu-
sion, deceit—mowed down, impaled. When he
finishes, he laughs so loud that God has to cover
His ears.

I have a few hours' sleep, but I manage to get to school with a first draft of my play. At lunchtime I meet my Theater of Truth. Their faces are excited and eager and probably for the first time they feel part of a group, feel they have a purpose. I can't disappoint my dregs.

"Well, you know how the other theater group is doing *South Pacific.* How about we send it up? We'll call it *South Pacific Two.* It's a sequel. And it's a rap musical."

"So what's the plot?" one dreg asks.

I tell them. "It's five years later. Nellie Forbush is bored with her marriage. She begins an affair with Liat's brother Kiat. Meanwhile, her husband, Emile, devotes his time to getting rich. He opens up hotels which bring in planeloads of tourists, factories which spew pollution, and he pays the natives low wages—barely enough to survive."

"Yes, and the natives are restless."

"Definitely. Bloody Mary starts a revolution."

"Bloody Mary gets bloody."

"Factories are burned. The island is in flames. But Emile, who has become president, brings in the troops and thousands are killed. Kiat is killed. Nellie, overwrought with grief, shoots Emile. And in the end a tidal wave drowns the beautiful island of Bali H'ai. A tidal wave brought on by global warming caused by pollution spewed out by Emile's factories."

"When can we start rehearsal?" one eager beaver asks.

"After school."

"Where will we meet?"

"We'll meet at the King's Food Court."

My dregs are ebullient. Suddenly they look like winners and movers and shakers, not tired feeble shadows lurking in crevices where I found them.

AUTUMN WEDDING

I take Leah out to the park to crunch the autumn leaves. Elsinore has a lot of European trees, and it's quite spectacular during the autumn month of April. We find ourselves a nice spot under a tree and sit on the brown and orange carpet of fallen leaves. A few hundred yards away a wedding is taking place before a flaming red tree. Men in tuxes and women in silken gowns mingle in circles, waiting for the bride to come. A musical quartet tunes up their instruments. A boy plays with an empty baby stroller, pushing it around like a motorcar.

"I bumped into your dad a few days ago," she says to me. "He told me he's lost his job."

I wish she hadn't mentioned him. I suddenly go gloomy. He failed because I failed him. Why, what an ass am I. Here I am, enjoying myself with my girlfriend, while that bastard Claude is at home screwing my mum, and my dad's burning away in his own hell. I am so pigeon hearted. My dad once rescued me when I was at the beach and I got caught in a rip. Now he's in a rip and I do nothing. Nothing! Just yak, blah, mutter, ramble my heart away like a telemarketer.

A lame pigeon limps along, pecking the grass for food.

I make a comment. "I wonder how long he'll survive. Nature's not kind to frailty."

"Maybe he has a partner to look after him."

"Maybe his partner's divorced him, found herself another pigeon, stronger, more virile, more reliable, more rich."

"Yeah," she says with growing annoyance, "and has a Porsche, blah, blah, blah. Do you have to anthropomorphize nature? I'm sure Nature is cruel, but I don't think she's bitter and twisted."

"You think I'm bitter and twisted?"

"Yeah, you twist everything you see and twist everything I say. Like I can't talk to you without you putting some innocent remark I've made into something sinister."

She stands up angrily and ready to burst into tears. "I'm sick of you. You make me feel ugly and horrible."

I chase after her and grab her arm. She shoves me away. "Go away. Why . . . why do you hate me so much?"

I hold her tight and she begins to cry.

"You don't know me . . ." she mutters tearfully. "You think you do . . . but you don't . . . You're always judging me . . . but you're wrong . . . You make me out as someone so terrible . . ."

I notice that the wedding has started, and the bride and groom are standing together before the celebrant.

"Do you ——— take this woman to be your lawful wife, to love and to honor, to comfort and respect, through sickness and through health, for richer or poorer?"

I grasp her tight.

The wedding guests cheer and clap. For the newly wedded couple, not us.

ART TRAP

Night of the premiere of *South Pacific Two*. I greet the audience as they come in. Mum and the ever-smiling Claude congratulate me. Professor Polly wishes me luck. Leah is radiantly beautiful in her black gown. I escort her to our seats. I turn to see where Principal Polly is and where my mum and Claude are. I want to see their reaction. My play will catch them out, reveal the foulness of their life. This is what art is all about: holding up a mirror to the ugly soul of humanity. I foresee what my play will do. Nothing less than a revolution. Principal Polly will apologize to the whole school. Mum, shocked at her filthy, vulgar lust, will return to my dad. Out of honor, Claude will commit suicide. The power of Art.

"You look very excited, Matt," says Leah.

"I am. Today is the end of all lies."

"And the beginning of your artistic career," she says proudly.

"Shall I sit on your lap?" I ask Leah.

"Usually I sit on your lap. Isn't that how it works?" she whispers seductively into my ear.

"Tonight I can perform miracles."

The lights dim and the curtains rise up. A girl in a sailor's outfit comes out on the stage. The drum and bass start blasting away. Some of the audience cover their ears from the aural onslaught.

> *"Yo, I'm Nellie Forbush*
> *I used to be a cockeyed optimist*
> *Now I'm a rabid pessimist*
> *I was a dope for hope*
> *Now I need dope to cope*
> *I was in love*

With a most wonderful guy
Now I can't stand 'im—
I wish I could leave 'im—
I could even kill 'im
Now I'm looking for thrills
So gimme some
Younger-than-springtime boys
I wanna smash their innocence
Relieve my vehemence
Life is too short anyway
To be burdened by morality
Sex is pure simplicity
Love is too complexity
So I wanna get some
Younger-than-springtime boys."

Nellie Forbush joins three Balinese boys in a provocative, erotic dance. I glance toward Mum. She seems to be thinking. Have I cast a mirror into her prurient heart? I then glance at Professor Polly. He no smile. Hee-hee. The mouse is in the trap. I am breaking the neck of hypocrisy. The power of Art.

Then Nellie's lover does his rap.

> *"My name is Kiat*
> *Liat's my sis*
> *She was hopin'*
> *Lieutenant Cable would be able*
> *To support her financially.*
> *But he's dead unfortunately*
> *So she's looking for another rich honkie*
> *Who's looking for hanky-panky*
> *This island paradise*
> *Used to belong to no one*
> *And used to feed every one*
> *Now whitey has taken everythin'*
> *So we ain't got nothin.'*
> *I'm Nellie's joy boy*
> *Her body sweatshop toy*
> *Tho she's rather stingy*
> *Pays me stinky wagey*

She gives me
A buck for a fuck
A buck for a fuck!"

"Lights! Lights!" Professor Polly explodes. "This show is over!"

The parrot strides to center stage and apologizes to the audience, especially the shocked mums and dads. The younger audience boo him. He makes a beeline for me.

"Matt, I'd like to have a word with you backstage."

THE PARROT'S REVENGE

Principal Polly takes me to the teacher's toilet to speak to me—it being the only place in the vicinity where he can speak to me in private. Symbolically speaking, it seems apt.

The parrot is bristling. If he had a beak he'd bite off my nose.

"What do you think you are doing?"

"Satire."

"That wasn't satire. That was obscene. Rodgers and Hammerstein would be turning in their graves."

"My play wasn't obscene. I was holding up a mirror to the obscenity of our society."

Principal Polly shakes his head. "You are part of society. If you are going to go against it, you will be punished. Society will spurn you and marginalize you."

"That doesn't bother me."

"I was an idealist like you. I thought I could change the world. But the world doesn't want to change, it wants you to change. Whatever happened to the hippies of the sixties? They are now the establishment and they have not changed the world a whit. You can't change the world."

"'Things rank and gross in nature possess it merely,'" I quote.

"Shakespeare's *Hamlet*. Let me remind you that Hamlet dies in the end. He could have eventually become the king of Denmark, married Ophelia, lived happily ever after, but he threw it all away."

"But he accomplished meting out justice."

Polly sighs.

"I can't stop you from wanting to change the world. But I can't have you using four-letter words in our school auditorium. If you don't remove those words, I won't permit your play to be shown."

"You won't allow any four-letter words in our play."

"Yes."

"So four-letter words like 'that' or 'love' I've got to remove?"

"You know what I mean."

"So if I changed 'A buck for a fuck' to 'A buck for a duck' you'd be happy?"

"Yes."

"Even though it doesn't make sense."

"You can change the story. That Balinese boy,

instead of being a gigolo, can be a duck seller. You'd still be making the same point."

"Yes, and maybe Nellie enjoys having sex with ducks."

"Matt, you don't need to be filthy to be witty. Take comedians like Bob Hope. He didn't resort to innuendos and filth. Do you think his career would have lasted as long if he wasn't wholesome?"

"Thank you for your advice. I shall consider a career in wholesome comedy. Meanwhile I'll discuss the four-letter words with my fellow thespians."

"Don't discuss them. Get rid of them."

"Have you eyes?"

"I beg your pardon?"

"Eyes. Do you have them? If you do, then how can you be blind to the suffering, the ugliness, the injustice around you?"

"Matt, don't look too far away. Or you might forget to look at yourself."

I want to say it out loud. Joker wants me to say it. *Go on. Tell him to his face: "Fuck you, Polly!"*

Like a sonic boom that would break all the windows in Elsinore High.

But I have a theatrical troupe that depends on me. Maybe they want to continue performing the show without the offending words.

"Fff . . . fine, Mr. Paul."

Later, I speak with my players. Brave souls, they refuse to compromise. The scandal has made them heroes. They say they'll take my play to some stage, maybe a garage, or the streets. The Theater of Truth lives on. The Theater of Compromise it will not be.

LESS ART, MORE MATTER

SCENE: Outside Leah's home. Strong winds are shaking and rustling the leaves on the trees and the ground. Fast-moving clouds sail past the half-moon.

I look straight into Leah's eyes. "Are you honest?"

She doesn't blink or glance away. "You know I'm

always honest with you."

"Whose side are you on? Your dad's or mine?"

"I don't agree with his decision to stop the play."

I kiss her on the cheek and start walking home.

She calls after me. "What about your play? What are you going to do with it?"

I turn to her. "It's dead as far as I'm concerned."

"Are you just going to give up that easily?"

"That's the business of Art. If a publisher doesn't want to publish your book, if a record company doesn't want to produce your record, them's the breaks."

"Matt, Art is not just a business. It's also what you are. You're an artist, Matt. Don't give up on that."

MUDDY-METTLED RASCAL

I feel like a complete idiot. How did I delude myself into thinking that I could change anything? I'm

125

depressed and inconsolable. My cell phone rings, but I don't answer it. I just want to be alone. That's all there is. Being alone. Who is Leah? Just an image in my head. Does she exist outside me? I don't know her other than what I think of her. When I close my eyes the world disappears.

I begin to tremble and shake. I notice my bedroom has turned into mud. I fall off my bed and immerse myself in the rising mud. I laugh and cry and laugh and cry.

Joker lives in a world of mud. Nothing grows here. A snake winds itself around him. Rats and cockroaches crawl around him. We are all foul creatures, full of venom and misery. God, seeing how ugly the world was, packed up and left. The angels couldn't bear the stench. They have abandoned this vile stinking world to the devils.

MINE EYES TO MY VERY SOUL

When I step out of my bedroom I see my mum. She just smiles, and that really annoys me and sparks me off. I grab her shoulders and push her to the wall. "I'm sick of your smiles. Why don't you ever talk to me?"

She looks frightened. "You're hurting me, Matt!"

"You've hurt me much more."

"I never meant to—"

I let it all out like a volcano. "Do you know why you hurt me? Why didn't you comfort me when I was hurting? Why did you treat me like I was a stranger? Just because you divorced Dad did not mean you divorced me as well. I'm still your son. You cut me off. I can understand you leaving Dad but I don't understand that you didn't reach out to me, talk honestly to me, explain. I needed you but you weren't there for me. Instead, you flaunted and rammed your Claude down my throat! You made me think love was something deceitful and vulgar and monstrous. All I wanted from you was a word or touch or gesture to reassure me that love wasn't my enemy."

My mum is crying. "I'm sorry, Matt . . . but I've never been good at talking things out . . . I knew you weren't happy about the divorce, but I couldn't explain myself to you . . . You say I treated you like a stranger, but I'm a stranger to my heart . . . I—I—"

But she won't say she loves me, so I leave her and run out of the house.

DAMNED GHOST

I decide to visit my father, the ghost. His apartment is a sty, with unwashed dishes and empty beer bottles lying around. I'm both shocked and sad. I believe that a person's home is a reflection of his soul. If this was his soul, then it was a real mess. We sit on sofas facing each other, like we were on a TV interview show.

"Dad, you have to take better care of yourself."

He catches me looking around, but it doesn't seem to bother him—the state he is living in. "I guess I have to, since I don't have your mum to do the cleaning up for me."

"Don't you think it's about time you move on? Forget her. You're a good-looking bloke. You'll find someone in no time."

His face doesn't register any optimism. "I'm just useless. No bloody use to anybody."

"That's not true. Why don't you get a new job? You have a lot of experience."

"I'm obsolete. Past my use-by date."

"Don't be negative, Dad."

"I knew my days in the corporate world were numbered when my company hired some young blokes and I couldn't understand their lingo. It was English, all right, but with lots of fancy business jargon. I am a straight talker, but everybody talks spin nowadays. Everyone's spinning like a cricket spin bowler. The spinners are taking over the world. Guys like Claude, who could charm his way into any woman's arms. Or rather, my wife's arms. The bastard!"

I don't respond, feeling he just wants to talk.

"It's all my fault. I let Gertrude drift from me. I saw it happening and I didn't do anything. I should have been more affectionate, more romantic even. But I never, ever thought she'd end up leaving. And she had loved me. When we got married she adored me like I was a pop star. And where is all that love now? Gone. And yet I still love her and will always love her. Where did her love for me go, Matt?"

I want to tell him that Mum stopped loving me too, but I keep quiet.

"It hurts so much knowing that she doesn't love me anymore," he says, tears trickling down his cheeks.

"Stop beating yourself up, Dad."

"I should have fought tooth and nail to save my marriage. But I did nothing. I stood back and let it happen. I couldn't lift a finger. Now I'm letting myself slide and slide into god knows what."

Suddenly he is aware of my presence. He sees something in me like he was peering into my soul. "Matt, you have my genes. You are weak, too. I've heard that you're flunking school. Like me, you've lost control. Listen to me, Son. Don't do what I did. Take control of your life. Don't let the weakness inside you take over. Fight for your life. Fight for your happiness. Fight for love."

"I will, if you will."

But these are just words to him. He takes a swig from the bottle. My dad is not going to change his life. As he said, he is a weak man.

And so am I.

Joker is waiting for me with a knife in his hand. I query him and expect him to laugh at any moment, but he stares hard into my eyes. There is no light or joy in them, just something cold and terrifying. He gives me the knife and I take it without even think-ing about it.

MY THOUGHTS BE BLOODY

When I get home I find Claude by himself. My mum is in her bedroom. He is friendly and eager to bond with me. He doesn't realize I'm going to bond with him with a knife I had hid in my jacket.

We share a beer together in the living room. I hope the beer will cancel my conscience. No more time for thoughts, just swift bloody action.

"You've made your mother very unhappy," he says to me.

"Then you'd better go to the bedroom and make her happy," I reply sarcastically.

"Matt, I know that you resent me for breaking up your parents' marriage."

"All is fair in love and war. You saw, you conquered."

"No, it's not like that. I'm not that kind of guy who goes around stealing other men's wives. It was only after Gertrude told me that she was leaving her husband that . . . You know what I mean. Before that we were just very good friends. Matt, I really love your mum and she loves me too. I feel like she's my soul partner. Don't you feel like that with Leah? You and she were meant to be together."

I say nothing, downing the last drop of beer.

I feel the hilt of my weapon. *Seize the moment*, I tell myself.

But the moment came and went and I put my hands in my lap.

I can't kill him. Not because I believe in one slippery word he said. But because it won't stop my mum from loving him and make her love me and my dad. Love obeys nobody but itself.

At that moment my mum comes out. I stand up

and go to her. She looks frightened, thinking I'm going to punch her. Instead I hold her. "I love you, Mum." I haven't said that to her for a long time. And probably the last time. But I know now that I can't hurt her.

She is speechless, perhaps too shocked.

Then I rush away, out of the house, for I know I won't ever see her again.

ACT 4

SOMETHING
IS ROTTEN

ROCKET TO THE STARS

I have to get away from Joker.

Joker says to me, "You need me."

"No, I don't."

"I am what makes people great. I am the genius in the human soul. I will save you from a life of mediocrity."

"You're trying to destroy me."

"That's because I am powerful. I will destroy you if you aren't strong enough."

"Just tell me this. Are you good or are you evil?"

"You just don't understand me." He grins, quite mischievously.

I wonder if I keep on walking whether I'll reach the edge of the earth. Elsinore is quiet and empty of humans, all of whom are inside their boxes. Up above, bats are flying. I can hear catfights and dogs barking.

I decide to visit Ray. I haven't visited him since . . . the funeral. I ain't superstitious, believing that the only place to visit a soul is at the cemetery. But I want something solid, instead of talking to him in my head. I get so trapped in my head, tangled up in words.

The cemetery hosts tombs going over a century back, so it combines new shiny tombstones with old brown scary ones. A Frank Sinatra song is jangling out of a CD player. A couple of gravediggers are waist deep in a freshly dug hole.

"Who's the new tenant?" I ask them.

"A Mr. Rick Yo," the older one answers.

"Rick Yo, no kidding. Not the grade school teacher?"

He nods. "That's the unlucky fellow."

"What did he die of?"

"Life. He had enough of it so he gassed himself in

his car in the garage. I hope the Lord Almighty will accept him. He don't look too kindly on suicides."

The younger man, who looks like a younger version of the older man, sniggers. "He's heading nowhere but a hole in the ground."

"A bloke deserves much more than a hole in the ground after all the sweats and knocks."

The young mocker answers back, "A hole in the ground is all he gets and that's plenty enough space for someone who won't do much moving around."

The old man crosses himself. "I'd like to think Mother Mary will give us all a big hug and a kiss when she greets us."

"I'd like to give her a kick—"

"Oy!" he yells at the youth. "No blaspheming around here, Son. There are some dead Catholics among us."

The young man laughs with scorn. "My dad reckons the dead can hear and that they like listening to Frank Sinatra. Just crumbling bones and rotting guts—that's what the dead are."

I leave them, startled by the suicide of my old schoolteacher. I never gave a thought whether he was happy or not. He was just a teacher. But we are all human after all.

Alas, poor Rick Yo, I knew him barely. I liked him; he was funny and kind. He deserves better than a hole in the ground. He was no monster, but then maybe God is a monster.

I locate Ray's grave, which is blanketed with fallen leaves, and squat down to touch the granite slab on the ground. It feels funny, him lying here. His bedroom was like a second home to me. That's where he ought to be buried, with rock music blasting out of the speakers. I spent hours in there with him, chatting and arguing all things on heaven and earth.

I lie back on his plot, gazing up at the great big black starry sky above. I don't know what to expect coming here. Maybe Ray can give me some answers, he was a bright fellow.

I realize that I never did get a proper chance to

grieve for my friend. A few weeks after his funeral came my mum's wedding, with the same priest and same caterer. My heart was sobbing and spewing and spinning this way and that until it burst into flames.

O Ray, can you speak to me one last time?

But all I hear is Frank Sinatra crooning "Come Fly with Me."

So I scream like Edvard Munch's painting.

After a while I get up and leave. I have no idea what to do or where to go. Maybe to Leah? I'm so confused. I'm lost. I can't make a choice. This or that or there.

Glancing up, I see the moon. But it's Joker's face. I remember my knife and aim it at the white, mocking face.

"What do you want?" I scream up at him.

A car pulls up beside me.

The Tin Man. Has Joker sent him to me?

I hop inside. I'm feeling fatalistic—let Joker take me where he wants to take me. I'm just a speck of dust in this dancing cosmos.

"Where you going?" he asks me.

"Nowhere."

"That's where I'm heading."

"Let's get out of Elsinore as fast as we can."

"Okay." Brad puts his foot on the accelerator and we blast our way out of this hick town. Maybe I won't come back. I'm on a rocket to the stars. I am Spaceship Matt on a secret mission. I close my eyes and sleep.

JOKER THE FOOL

The dogs are barking. Watch out, Joker. Oops, too late. Joker falls into a hole. He clambers up and dusts himself off. Only three strides before he slips on a banana peel. Ouch! He rubs his sore bottom. A sucker for punishment, he gets up again and walks, even though he doesn't know where he is going. He is

going somewhere, anywhere, nowhere. The dogs are
barking again—watch out! He falls over the cliff. Oh
dear, what a silly fellow is Joker. Don't get up, but he
gets up. There's a long road ahead . . .

OR

When I wake up it is daylight. The road is a slick silver knife plunging into the bare midriff of the horizon. Cows and sheep dot the fields like plastic toys. I don't know where I am and that makes me glad. I want to forget the past. Seek a new identity.

The road brings different vistas and possibilities. We go straight, up, over, round.

"Pull over. Nature calls."

The Tin Man parks on a dirt strip beside some bushland. We get out and pick our own trees. We are two stray dogs.

I glance up at my tree and then notice the empty

blue sky. Only a few fluffy white clouds here and there.

I bark and howl. So does Brad. *Woof-woof-woof! Awooooooh!*

We zip through small towns not unlike Elsinore. We are going so fast that the road can't keep up with us.

"So what about Leah?" Brad asks me. "You broke up with her?"

"I don't know. I think I want her to break up with me."

"You got brains, looks, money—you can accomplish anything. Yet you're in a car with a deadbeat like me. All I can look forward to is a jail term. You're mad."

"I've done with success. Now I want to succeed in failure."

"You still want to kill your stepfather?" he asks me.

"I ain't no killer. That I know."

"Well, isn't that a fact."

Come evening Brad pulls up at a gas station.

"You have money?" he asks me.

"No. Do you?"

"No." He bends and reaches under his seat and takes out a gun and hands it to me.

"After I fill the car up you go in there and stick up the guy."

"Are you kidding?"

"Look, if you want to survive on your own and not have your mummy and daddy look after you, you have to do whatever it takes to survive."

"I can't do it."

"Don't think about it. Do it." He gets out of the car and takes out the gas hose to fill up the car.

Once again I'm given a gift from the dark gods, tempting me, luring me to the other side. Just do it. Don't think about it. I think too much and where has it gotten me?

Brad bangs on the side window as he walks past and strides inside the gas station. He picks up a plastic basket and begins to throw groceries inside it. He glares at me to hurry.

But I can't stop thinking. Thinking about the consequences. Thinking what will happen. Thinking about my victim.

I was born to think. What's wrong with that? The dark, thoughtless world of Brad isn't for me.

Joker is seated like a Buddha on the hood, facing me. He puts forward his two fists, clutching something. "To be or not to be? Leah or not Leah? Good or Evil? Yes or No? Stay or Go?"

I nod. Life is about choices. Good or evil? I know I can't be evil.

Suddenly Brad bursts out of the station and jumps in the car and quickly pulls the car away and screeches to the open road. I twist my head and see the gas station owner chasing after us.

"I think he's taking down the license plates."

"That's all right. It's not my car."

He grins, then he stops grinning. "You left me hanging out there. Why didn't you go in?"

"I just couldn't do it."

"You're chicken. Useless. You deserve to die."
He takes the gun from me and points it at my head
and pulls the trigger.

I jerk as if I could avoid a bullet at point-blank.
But the gun's empty.

"You're crazy!" I yell furiously at him.

He laughs. He points the gun at his temple and
squeezes the trigger. "You've taken the wrong ride."

LEAH 2

We espy a female, strolling down an empty road,
carrying a large bag half her size and her right thumb
sticking out for a hitch.

"Hey," Brad says, leering at the girl. "We can
have us some fun."

I don't like what he means by fun, but he has
pulled over and offers her a ride. She, a young girl
with pale skin and short jet-black hair, looks at Brad

and hesitates, but when she sees me I can tell she trusts me. She gets in the back.

"Hi, my name's Leah."

I do a double take.

How funny! Maybe she's the right Leah for me. Leah 2. Fate has brought her to me. Life is but a stage and we all play our scripted roles.

"Where are you going?" I ask Leah 2. I think I'll call her Lia, to avoid confusion.

"To the big city."

"We'll take you there." I turn to Brad to see if he doesn't mind. He doesn't.

"What are you guys doing?" she asks.

"Nothing," I answer. "A couple of nobodies with nothing to do and nothing to look forward to going nowhere."

"Oh yeah. Been there, done that, didn't like it. I prefer to go somewhere."

"You must be somebody then."

"I'd like to be somebody."

"A singer, right?" I ask.

"Can't sing a note."

"An actress."

"No way. Though I've been known to be a drama queen."

"So what kind of somebody do you wanna be?"

"I dunno. I want to first get a job, then try to go to university, maybe art school. Who knows?"

"And I guess your parents don't approve?"

"Bingo. My parents are dead set against me being myself. That's why I'm leaving home. So I can be myself."

"A runaway."

"I prefer to call myself a goer. I'm going to where I wanna go."

A NOBODY IN NOWHERE LAND

We stop at a small town, which has a giant statue of a meat pie with tomato sauce. The sight of it makes us hungry, so we pull up at a local milk bar and Leah 2 or Lia shouts us some food in exchange for our ride. I get myself a meat pie, not as large as the statue of course, while Brad gets himself a burger with the works and Lia some chips soaked in vinegar and salt.

We sit ourselves on a bench near the town hall, with Lia sandwiched between Brad and me.

"You don't talk much," Lia says to Brad.

"Words have never been much use to me."

"He's a man of action and I'm a man of words," I say.

"That's all right. I like words. I like to play with them sometimes like poetry."

Brad laughs as if poetry is the dumbest thing to do.

"That's why I want to be an artist. Which is about honesty, stripping one's self of illusions, humanity."

"I'd rather be a car," says Brad, joking. *"Vroom vroom."*

"What about you, Matt?" she asks me.

"I want to be nobody."

"A nobody in nowhere land. I don't believe you. Are you telling me that you have no talent or intelligence or ability whatsoever? You don't want to use your talents?" she interrogates me.

I don't answer her. I think my talent is making everyone including myself miserable.

LITTLE BIRD

The hour is late so we drive into some sparse bushland and set up camp to sleep. Lia sets up her spot in the back of the car, Brad on the hood, and myself on the grass.

I wake up when I hear a girl shouting. "Get off me! I'm not interested! Get off me!"

She runs out of the car and kneels by my side. "Will you protect me?"

I look at Brad, grinning.

"What's your problem? How do you think you'll

survive in the city. You'll be selling your body soon enough."

"I'll never be a prostitute. Never!"

"You will."

"Let's take a walk," Lia asks me.

I don't want to get up, but she keeps nudging me.

We run into open pasture. A herd of cows is snoozing on their hooves. Lia, turning to me, puts her hush finger to her mouth and we creep quietly between the snoozing cows.

We weave through the herd and scramble up a slope and rest on the drought-parched grass.

I sit beside her.

"All I want is to be free, but there are always assholes that won't let me."

"You mean Brad?"

"Yeah, and like my parents. I couldn't breathe anymore in that house. My parents were suffocating me—do this, do that. They wouldn't even let me have my own CDs. I have a little bird inside me and I have to set it free."

Somehow her words make me think about my mum. Maybe all she did was break free from my dad, who was holding her back. Just moving forward. Setting her bird free.

"A penny for your thoughts."

"Worth less than that."

"Tell me."

"Just thinking about my mum, my girlfriend. Females—I can't figure them out."

"What I think—we all have our destinies and ultimately we're all on our own."

"You think so?"

"Yeah. Tell me about your girlfriend."

I laugh. "She has the same name as you."

"Really!"

"Weird, huh? But she's different from you—shy, conservative."

"You love her?"

"I think we're growing apart."

I gaze into Lia's face and realize the uncanny resemblance to Leah. Except for the black hair and paler skin. It's as if Leah was disguising herself for a role in a movie.

"Why don't you leave her? You ever think maybe she's not right for you?"

"I'm changing while she hasn't."

"Changing—what do you mean?"

"I'm moving and she's stationary. I don't know where I'm moving to, but I just can't stay where I was."

"That's exactly why I'm leaving home. I just can't stay where I was. We have an appointment with destiny. Do you love her?" she asks me seriously.

I think about it for a while. She has forgotten she had asked the question when I finally answer. "Yes. I'm like my father. My mum's divorced him, but he continues to love her. Me and my dad don't fall out of love easily."

"That's great. I wouldn't mind a guy loving me like that one day. But not now. Because I'm so in love with myself at the moment. I want to devote my time to bringing out the best in me."

"So love's off limits to you."

"I don't mind if a guy loves me a little bit. You want to love me a little bit?" She rests her hand on mine.

"I can't love a little bit. I can only love a lot."

She withdraws her hand. "That's way too much for me right now." She turns to lie on her stomach and closes her eyes.

I lie down beside her. I feel like an idiot, not making a move on a pretty girl. I guess I'm love's idiot. Leah's fool. But what is it about love that makes me love Leah and not Lia? It can't be purely physical because they resemble each other. I guess love happens underground, deep within.

Lia and I lie down, clasped in each other's arms. When I start shaking, she rubs me with her arm and soothes me to sleep.

When we get back to the car early in the morning Brad has gone. Lia's things are strewn all over the grass. Actually, Brad has made a face with them, the smile a string of her colored undies.

"That bastard!" Lia screams, bending to pick up her clothes.

"Well at least he didn't steal your stuff."

She quickly rifles through her bag, takes out her wallet, and checks it. "Money's still there."

"You see, he's not really bad. He's just got a tough exterior."

"Yeah, I'd like to take a kick at his tough exterior ass."

I pick up a note wrapped around some paper money. It reads, *Matt, I couldn't wait. Must get back to Elsinore. Here's some cash—ha, I had cash after all to pay for gas and groceries—just in case you need it. Mate, hope you'll find in Sydney what you're looking for. Elsinore's too small for the likes of you.*

So he had cash all that time. He didn't need to rob the gas station. He just wanted to test me. Or push me. Push me into doing something rash and reckless. He wants me to play his game. What are the stakes? Leah?

I won't play his game.

I have a bird inside me that wants me to go to Sydney, my mission seems to be compelling me to go there.

I remember a newspaper story about a Czech who always wanted to visit Sydney, scraped and stinted to pursue his dream down under. Years of hard work and sacrifice finally brought him to his goal. A dream comes true. A week after arriving as he strolled down a street in Woolloomooloo, admiring the blue gem of Sydney Harbor, a stranger with an axe pounced on him and opened his head like a grotesque flower.

I must go to Sydney. Maybe a man with an axe is waiting for me.

THE BRIDGE

We hitch a ride on a semi to Sydney. The first thing Lia wants to do is to climb the arch of the Sydney Harbor Bridge. I ain't exactly eager, but we trek all the way through the city, not dillydallying anywhere, as she is determined not to do anything else. I want lunch, but, no, the bridge must be conquered first. My stomach must wait.

When we arrive at the foot of the bridge tower we head to the tourist office that arranges the bridge walks. We suit up in a special costume that has metallic rings to slide the ropes through, harnessing us so a bullying wind won't be tipping us over into the harbor. A chain gang of eight other tourists, German and Japanese, join us.

Only when I start the ascent do I discover that I have a fear of heights. There being no mountains or skyscrapers in Elsinore, I can't have known this. But I ain't so freaked out that I panic and scream and cry. Instead, I concentrate on watching Lia's ass as she ascends ahead of me. I refuse to look up or down. Just blinkered on her ass. Lia striding along, bravely taking in the panoramic view of the city.

I wonder if a person's derriere characterizes their personality. Lia's ass is firm, jaunty, and confident. She has an ass that carries her forward. I reflect on my Leah's ass. Hers is feminine and elegant, but has gravity. It is an ass that gives her balance. But not an ass to climb bridges or run away to the city. An ass of a splendid statue.

I follow Lia's sassy ass all the way to the summit. She turns to me, beaming.

"This is so beautiful, Matt."

I don't want to appear scared so I brace myself, gripping the rails, and take a glance at the views. My eyes trace the harbor snaking its way toward the ocean, which lines the horizon.

"Don't you want all this?" Lia asks me.

"No," I answer truthfully. Altogether, Sydney resembles a junkyard.

"I want it. I belong in this city. Good-bye, country bumpkin. Hello, city girl."

WHAT A RIOT

I am exhausted when we reach sea level. But Lia is still brimming with energy. She is a tornado ripping through the city.

We stumble straight into an antiglobalization protest outside the stock exchange. It comes as no surprise to me that Leah 2 is also ready to take on the might of the capitalist world.

The protest has not begun; the protesters, milling about casually like at a party. Some holding up placards, banners, and effigies. A very tall muscly man, painted green, has dressed up as the Incredible Hulk. He holds up a placard: I'M REALLY REALLY PISSED OFF WITH THE WTO.

Guarding the stock exchange is a phalanx of police officers in riot gear, standing at ease or on horseback.

These two opposing sides make great contrasts. While the protesters are ragged and motley, the police look homogeneous. I observe closely the faces of the police. They chat affably among themselves and don't look like monsters. Yet one feels afraid of them; their rigidity and stillness exude professionalism. Their job is to protect, defend, maintain order, and execute their orders with brutal efficiency. Yes, they are human, but their training will make them respond inhumanly. So I'm wary as we're about to wake up the sleeping giant.

I can see Lia is rather incensed at the sight of the blue police officers. They probably represent to her the cold and harsh authority of her parents. She wants to lash out, challenge them, and hurl abuse at them.

Then a man stands up on a soapbox with a megaphone. I slowly recognize the man—Osric, the ex-clown.

I laugh, for I know it's Joker, disguised as Osric. Because he winks at me when he sees me.

"To protest or not to protest, that is the question. Do we sit on our asses and watch reality TV or do we get off our asses and engage reality? Reality is not a TV show. Reality is two billion people in poverty. Reality is the obscene trillion-dollar arms trade. Reality is the giant ozone hole. Reality is the depletion of the fishing stock in the world's oceans. Reality is this world we live in and it belongs to us all and not to the rich and powerful. Reality is the truth, and not the lies and spin and deceit that stunt and smother and cocoon us. This stock exchange pretends that it owns and runs the world. It does not. This is our world! This is our world! Let's fill this hollow building with our souls and our humanity!"

The protesters, including me, feel galvanized. We want to change the world! This is our mission: let the world be ruled with love and wisdom!

We begin to surge forward toward the entrance of the stock exchange. The police quickly react and push us back with their shields. The two sides are getting angry and more determined. The preceding calmness has disappeared. Then scuffles break out as police try to arrest a few protesters . . . Horses charge forward . . . Protesters flee, with fear on their faces . . . Marbles are thrown under the hooves . . . A neighing horse slips and stumbles, bringing the rider down with it . . . Batons rise and fall viciously . . . blood streaming from a man's forehead . . . Everybody's yelling.

"Get your trotters off me, pig!"

"Get a job, hippie!"

"Fascists!"

"Freaks!"

Where is Lia? . . . Placards fly toward the stock exchange . . . I am caught in a human wave and it sweeps me toward the wall of officers . . . A baton crashes on my head   then the wave pulls me away . . . My legs are jelly . . . I fall down and I see legs all around me . . . I try to stand up . . . then I get pushed down . . . And a scrum of people collapses on me. I'm trying to breathe . . . forcing myself to breathe . . .

Bodies are yanked up by the police and hauled into vans . . . I gulp for oxygen . . . I scramble away, not wanting to get arrested . . . Smoke swirling around and it hurts my eyes . . . tear gas . . . The protesters are scattering . . . I quickly twist around to see where Lia is . . . I can't see her . . . But it is all chaos . . . The protesters are getting routed . . . The Incredible Hulk, pummeled by batons, is fighting back and lands a few punches . . . Then they tackle him to the ground and the police swarm on him.

"Lia!" I shout out. "Lia!"

A protester lights up the Australian flag and it bursts into flames . . . Faces of hatred, grief, despair . . . I touch my forehead and my palm is smeared in blood.

"Be brave!" Joker yells at me. "Courage is your only security. Or why don't you scurry into your little hole like a mouse?"

Joker charges at the front line, runs up someone's back and shoulders, and leaps upon the police like he was in a mosh pit.

Suddenly I am possessed with this black fury,

wanting to strike at the enemy. Time for debate is over; now is the time for fight. This world belongs to me and I will not be frightened away by guns. A human being is more than a sheep that eats and sleeps and blindly follows; he has honor and dignity and he must fight for his freedom. I don't feel afraid. I refuse to be afraid anymore. I know that ever since Ray died I had always felt this fear, this sense that life is truly frightening and sinister. I notice I'm shaking, but I resist it and charge toward the police.

As I run I nearly stumble on a young girl on her knees, distraught and in tears. I stop and hold out my hand to her. She takes it and I lead her away and off the street and onto the sidewalk.

"You're bleeding," she tells me, and takes out a handkerchief.

I kneel down and let her wipe the blood off with her pretty pink hanky. I am touched by her gesture. It also reminds me how I first met Leah.

"What's your name?" I ask her.

"Leah," she says.

I chuckle. Leah 3. Is Leah following me like a guardian angel?

"It's not a funny name."

"No, it's a beautiful name."

I smile at her. She smiles. I think about returning to the battle raging before me, but the young girl's smile right now seems so much more important to me. I have to return to Elsinore, my battle is there. Besides, before I deal with the rottenness of the world, I must deal with mine.

Joker is pushing a colored cart, hawking ice cream and cold drinks amid the smoke and shouts and cries and violence. Joker knows that all this isn't politics—this is just a sideshow, a circus. Politics is done behind many closed doors, deep inside the rotten heart, clogged with lies and corruption.

ISLAND

I head toward the city's exits. My eyes are stinging. All I can think of is escaping this ugliness.

"Matt!" a female voice calls behind me.

I turn and see Lia. She is unscathed, as if she had only been on a roller-coaster ride.

"You're hurt."

"I'm okay."

"Where are you going?"

"Home," I answer her.

"Why?" She stops and grabs me to look at her. "Stay here awhile. This is where it's all at. You're in the center of things. It's all at your fingertips—art, music, politics, and business. It's all here."

"I'm not even sure if I still have a home."

"You belong here . . . with me." It surprises me when I meet Lia's eyes. Her confidence slipping. Just a little.

"Maybe . . . later, I don't know."

"Let me know when you decide. Here's my cell phone number." She scribbles it down on a piece of paper and gives it to me. She kisses me, then leaves me. I envy her: she ain't afraid of the future. I keep walking. I reach Central Station and sit on a bench, unsure of what to do. I hate how my mood swings from up to down and back again. There's a monkey in my brain. I'm thinking about whether to go back to Elsinore or not. I think of taking a ship to a deserted island and living there à la noble savage. I'm sick of the world. The world won't miss me at all. I think of my mother, my father, Leah. I think of Lia. Leah or Lia? Lia doesn't want love, but Leah wants love at a price.

I don't do anything for a long while. North, south, west—it doesn't matter. It's all a big Nowhere to me.

I take out my cell phone. I need to speak to somebody, maybe Lia. I notice I have messages. One message is from Brad. *Matt, I'm going back to Elsinore. You don't deserve Leah. She needs a real man.*

I wonder if he's right.

There is another message from Leah.

> *matt, this is leah. where have u been? been trying
> to contact u. i organized a party 4 your theater
> group 2 perform. everybody came. friends, neigh-
> bors, students, even some teachers. everybody
> loved the show. i really admired your play. im
> beginning to understand what u r trying 2 do. u
> want the truth, u want justice. im on your side, ill
> always be on your side. c u l8er, i luv u.*

I smile and go buy a bus ticket to Elsinore. When
I think about it, I don't deserve Leah. But then, I
don't think she deserves Brad. He is one demon that
she wouldn't be able to tame. I can't allow him to
take her.

When I finally get on a bus, I fall asleep and
dream . . .

ACT 5

GOOD NIGHT, SWEET PRINCE

WHERE WILT THOU LEAD ME?

I draw open the curtains and enter a small room. It is dark except for the table, lit by a small desk lamp; Joker is seated, holding a pack of tarot cards. Joker cuts and shuffles the cards and spreads them out facedown before me. "Pick one," he tells me. "It's your future."

"What if I don't choose?" I say.

"That's a choice too," he answers.

IN THY ORISONS

I can't believe that beneath this patch of ground lies my Leah. Her blue eyes, her long brown hair, her lips—all dust. I want to speak to her and her to speak to me. Death is a wall. While I was gone she drowned in a troubled sea. Did she commit suicide? I know it was in her to do it. Whether she did or not, it was my fault. I wasn't around. Too busy thinking about myself.

A young man strides toward me. A well-built soldier. Her brother, Larry. I know what is coming. A hail of punches falls on me. I don't defend myself.

"You bastard! You killed my sister! She loved you and you drove her to this. I joined the army so I can fight terrorism, but I should have stayed here protecting my little sister from scum like you."

He kicks me while I lie crumpled on the ground. Perhaps he'll be kind enough to let me join Leah. However, he wants only to hurt me, not set me free. I know that this pain I feel will accompany me for the rest of my life.

CASUAL SLAUGHTERS

When I woke up I was in a house of blood. My hand was clasping a bloody knife. The last thing I remember was going out drinking with Brad. He must have spiked my drink, for I lost consciousness. He framed me for the murder of my mother and Claude. He framed me to have Leah for himself. In a way I deserve to be here. I planted the violent idea in his head and it bore fruit. My mother is dead and I'll never get the chance to love her like a son should.

I think of ending my life, but I realize that action would only hurt my father and my friends. I understand that what we do or think has consequences.

The cycle of pain must stop with me.

My only penance is to believe in life. When I get out of jail many years from now I will still be young enough to begin again. I will help people; I will give love and kindness. Maybe I can find a wife and start a family. I'll teach my children to love life. This is how I shall redeem myself. I can't bring my mother's life back, but I'll bring life back in me. I will enjoy life for her. I will be happy.

FUNERAL BAKED MEATS

Here I am, reincarnated as a fly, and I'm checking out my funeral. I buzz annoyingly among my mourners. Mum is crying, her face soaked in tears; Claude, who must have gained an extra ten kilos, tries to look downcast, but it's obvious he's can't wait for the wake so he can stuff himself with food and drink. I zoom straight into his nostril and he jolts and makes a funny face. I wriggle out of his nostril before he squishes me. Seated next to them is my dad who, although disconsolate, appears quite sober. Holding his hand is an elegant middle-

aged woman. His new girlfriend, I guess. Gotten over Mum I suppose. I see him casting sidelong glances at my mum. I guess not. I flit about and see Roscoe and Guildo. Guildo is asleep on Roscoe's shoulder, and I'm tempted to zip into his mouth. The priest who is performing the rites is dull and tedious. I see Principal Polly. I land on his nose and he goes cross-eyed for a sec. Beside him, slouched on her chair is Leah, smiling. Smiling! Then I realize Joker is seated next to her, whispering a joke into her ear.

As my coffin is lowered into the hole, Leah giggles. Suddenly she bursts out laughing. She rises, walks to the bier, and jumps in and lands on my coffin. Everybody stands up to look and finds her singing and tap-dancing! Polly pleads with her to get out of there. Then Guildo and Roscoe jump in, and they begin dancing on the coffin. Some of my classmates, like Bernie, want to join along, and in their rush push Claude into the hole.

But I'm just a fly past caring or even laughing.

My past life—Mighty Matt!—is fading from my memory. I find myself a fresh dog's turd and settle upon my feast. I've died and gone to heaven.

BLASTED WITH ECSTASY

You won't be able to tell that this scruffy obese man shuffling in the park, a man in his forties, although looking much older, was once a handsome young man, who had fine prospects. A prince in his time. He has spent the past twenty years in and out of work, not being able to find a job he enjoyed or cared for. Unmarried and without friends, he spends his time talking and arguing with himself. He lives in a rather small and squalid apartment, whose floor is strewn with old newspapers, sex magazines, and clothes. He is a hoarder of regrets and memories. Although still young enough to redeem himself, you can tell that he is stuck deep in a hole. A hole he started digging many years ago, back in high school, a hole of missed opportunities, a hole which has turned out to be a grave for his life.

BAD DREAMS INSIDE THE NUTSHELL

I rise up from the abyss of a nightmare. I turn to my wife, Leah, lying by my side. Being with her makes me feel secure and happy. The nightmare I had was that all I have was taken away from me— my wife, my kids, my home, my job, and my financial security.

But I know that my happiness will always be fragile, always on the verge of crumbling. There is no door or wall that can protect me and my family from the violent world outside. I am so scared, and every time I embrace my wife or my kids, I feel the chill that it could be the last time.

KING OF INFINITE SPACE

"Do you think Matt can hear us?" Leah asks the doctor. They are standing before Matt, who is seated facing the window.

"Probably not. He's lost in his fantasy world."

"Could he ever find his way back?"

"Who knows? He might come back today or maybe never."

"I hope he's happy."

"Perhaps."

She kisses this face that had eyes that don't look. "Good-bye, Matt."

Leah wishes she can do something or could have done something. She remembers how she caught Matt talking to himself. He told her he was talking to a fellow called Joker. She laughed it off, thinking he was just kidding. She didn't realize that Joker would consume him.

"Don't feel guilty, Leah," the doctor tells her.

"He didn't give up on you; he gave up on reality. It became too much to bear."

NIGHT AND DAY

I wake when the rooster crows. He wakes up the cows and sheep and the chickens in my small farm. I lie in bed until my body is ready to rise. I've got no job to rush to. I did write books once but not anymore. I've made enough money to buy this place in New Zealand. It's cold, windy, and isolated where I live. I like it that way. I want to be as far away as possible from civilization, which seems determined to destroy itself. I avoid reading the papers. There was a time I wanted to save the world, but that time has passed. You try to save the world and the world crucifies you.

I still write, but not for publication. When I write I write to God, whatever that is. God is that

companion I have when I take a walk in the coun-
tryside or by the sea. God is who I hear when I
hear the waves or the birds. God is the rain and
the wind that touch me. God is the silence inside
me, a silence that gets stronger.

I have dreamed about Leah again. I can't
understand why my heart has not forgotten her. It
seems that during the day my mind is in control,
while during the night my heart takes over. I
know that for the rest of this day I will not think
about her. I don't feel sad or lonely. But it seems
certain that when I close my eyes I will yearn and
cry for Leah.

QUINTESSENCE OF DUST

Burn, Paris, burn. Paris, the city of Love, is in flames.
The Arc of Triumph is now a rubble of defeat. The
Eiffel Tower is a charred skeleton. The Louvre has

been looted and vandalized. Mona Lisa's *enigmatic smile has been wiped off forever.*

A smart bomb has blown up Paris University and there are no more existentialists existing, and post-modernists are postmortem.

As the victorious soldiers and tanks march and roll through the streets, there is nobody greeting us with flowers. They cower inside their rooms. Although the inhabitants ought to be grateful. For we have liberated them from the tyranny of Love. We have removed the rotten heart of Love and cremated it. We have crushed and routed Love. Love will no more hurt or betray us. Love will no more burn or scorn us. Love will no more make fools of us all. Love will no more make us feel. Amore is now morte.

Hallelujah, hail the Lord of Loathing! Hatred will cleanse and purify us. Hatred will simplify the rainbow to black and white.

O Asteroid, please come, please smash this idiot planet, please, pretty, pretty please . . .

WORLD'S GONE HONEST

My twelve apostles had set up their Theater of Truth in an abandoned warehouse. At first the audiences were pitifully small, then word got round, and people trekked from country towns around Elsinore to watch. Some of those who came were inspired and set up their own Theater of Truth. Theaters cropped up from town to town. Then the virus of Truth spread to the cities. Then it traveled across the seas to New Zealand, then to Southeast Asia. It rolled across China, Russia, and Europe, then over the ocean to the Americas. It was an unstoppable bug. Art now belonged to the people; and people wanted the truth.

The truth! As the voters demanded the truth from them, politicians could no longer lie and deceive wantonly. Truth was an irresistible force. Because Truth demanded action, demanded solutions, politicians actually started doing their jobs of eradicating

poverty, wars, and pollution. Truth became so power-
ful that liars and deceivers were shunned and ostra-
cized. The spinners of the world could no longer
spin their deceitful webs.

A HIT, A VERY PALPABLE HIT

As usual, protesters greet my limousine. Everywhere
I go I'm booed and jeered. What people don't
understand is that politics is not about idealism. It's
about power. Pure and simple. I am prime minister
of Australia because I am very good at playing the
game. To be prime minister one has to have the
right backers—the big corporations, the media
tycoons. The corporations provide me the money,
and the media sells me to the voters; fortunately,
there are enough fools out there to vote for me.
That's politics. Don't enter politics if you want to
save the world. You enter politics because you are a

gladiator who is willing to crush all before him.

As I step out of the limousine it hit me. Right in the eye. I stagger back. My security desperately scramble to cover me. I reach for my eye, and I see yolk and broken shell spread all over my palm. How I loathe democracy!

BESTIAL OBLIVION

I married Lia. She wanted to be an artist but had to give it up when I got her pregnant. Like other married couples we take out a mortgage, have a couple of kids, and own a spoiled terrier. Bills pile up; my cholesterol rises; me and Lia pad on the pounds. We don't communicate; we watch TV. Sometimes we yell at each other; we yell at the kids; and the spoiled terrier yaps away. Teenage kids belt out heavy metal music in their bedrooms, which they

hide in and never come out. The noise never stops;
I fantasize about putting a bullet into my ears so I
can have some slice of silence, just peace and quiet,
for me, for me . . .

MATT THE GHOST

I'm a ghost.

I can't remember how I died. I know I was in a
bus, I had fallen asleep, and I was heading home.
But I didn't get to my destination.

Nightly I visit Leah's house. This is where I was
happy. There's no other place for me, so I must keep
coming back. This is my heaven so I am satisfied. I
hold her but I can't touch her. I talk to her but she
can't hear.

I watch her grow old. In spite of her sadness, she
never marries. She stayed faithful to me.

*In a way she's a ghost. She no longer exists in this
life. We're both waiting for the time we'll meet
again in another world less cruel.*

I'M BACK

The bus pulls up at Elsinore.

*I walk fast and excitedly. I want to fly straight to
her. At her house I knock on the door. Answering
the door is a woman in her late thirties.*

*Yet I recognize her immediately. Time has not
ravaged her. "Leah."*

She screws up her eyes. "No, it can't be. Matt."

"Yes." I want to hug her so much.

"It's been so long. What? Twenty years, maybe."

"Too long."

*"Why are you here?" she asks, blurting out the
first question she could think of.*

"I wanted to see you."

"Yeah. Well, here I am."

"You look beautiful."

"Thanks. Not bad for a middle-aged mother of two adolescent boys."

I look crestfallen. "I suppose you're married?"

"Yeah. Are you?"

"No. I've never . . ." But the words won't come out. That I've never loved anyone but her. And that I wished I had never left Elsinore without her. And all the successes that I had felt hollow and the relationships that I had gave me no true joy.

"How did you find me?"

I had lost her; and now I have found her. But does she want to be found?

I search her face, and know she doesn't love me anymore. That she has forgotten me in her heart.

Without saying good-bye, for I can't say it, I turn around and leave. I thought I had come home; but I am not meant to find a home. I get on the street which never ends.

BY THIS DECLENSION

I am falling, everything is black; I'm thrashing out my hands, trying to clutch or grab something. But there is nothing out there, just an eternal blackness, an infinite descent.

Suddenly in the darkness a light gleams. It looks like an angel, and in her hand a pink hankie, which she offers me.

It's Leah as a young girl when I first met her. Looking at her, it dawns on me that what she was offering was what I had been seeking all along. Her gesture of kindness and sympathy. What use is all the anger and sadness and confusion and turmoil if not to seek the joy and love waiting at the end? What's the purpose of the journey if there is no home to return to? What is the point of all thought when it cannot reach the conclusion that there is beauty in the heart of life?

I reach out for her pink hankie, but I'm falling

too fast. Soon there is no light anymore and it's just me and the darkness. This is how it feels to be totally alone, disconnected from everyone, from everything . . . this is hell.

THE BIRD OF DAWNING

I wake up from my deep sleep and burst out in tears. The thought of being permanently separated from Leah cuts me so deep. But it's not just for Leah. Tears flow for my mum, my dad, Ray, Roscoe, Guildo, Lia, and even for myself, because love hurts so much. Yet life without love is a black hole, a black hole I can no longer keep falling into. I need to believe in love. It gives me solid ground.

I have dreamed my futures. But which future do I pick? There are a million possible futures.

So what befalls me is partially up to me. Certain circumstances I'm not in control of. But what I'm in control of are the choices I make. Do I invite the darkness? Do I embrace the light? Every thought is a road; every action can inflict wounds on the way to victory or defeat.

I need to be with Leah. Maybe she'd leave me. Maybe I'm no good for her. Maybe we'd be better off with other partners. But then again maybe we'd be happy. I'm still young and I'm in love and the future seems so far away. The present belongs to her and me. That is all life can guarantee. All one can do is be brave in this scary world of ours. And keep the light alive in this world of darkness. When I see her I shall hold her and tell her that I love her and need her and ache for her. I don't want to be afraid of love. My mother and father loved each other once. But love cannot be kept or possessed. Love is a bird inside me. Crazy love, bursting with agony and ecstasy. But it makes the heart beat. Without love I am less than human.

Being human is about choices. Therefore I choose Love. I choose Leah. I choose Life. I choose Good.

I choose Wisdom. I choose Art. I choose Joker. His insanity keeps me sane. I want to laugh and share my laughter. The joke is that we don't know why we are here on this sad lonely rock, and the joke is all on us. Nobody knows.

I feel a certain peace. Or perhaps it's only a truce. The guns and bombs have gone silent inside me. I gaze out the window and enjoy the passing scenery. Such lovely cinematography!

When I arrive at Elsinore I fly to Leah's house.

Guess who answers the door?

The most beautiful girl in the world, and she has love in her eyes for me, just for me.

Ain't I a lucky guy?

I had been wrong about Leah. She loves me no matter what; through sickness or health; through poverty or richness; through winning or losing; through dumbness or smartness, through insanity, through sanity. It was I who failed her, judging her, condemning her. I am such a jerk.

"Where have you been, Matt?" she asks me.

"I've been lost in a black hole," I answer her. "But I'm back." I hug her; hug her so hard as if I were merging with her.

"I love you, Leah," I whisper to her. "Thanks for everything."

I'm grateful to Leah. The world should be grateful to all the Leahs that keep the light of love shining in its darkest days.

I close my eyes. A vision comes to me.

Leah and me are atop a burning building; smoke and fire encircle us; there is no hope for escape. But we are not afraid. We clasp hands and jump. But we don't fall, instead we rise, and we keep rising . . .

Love transcends gravity. Love is a bird.

Joker bursts out laughing at the absurdity of it all; then he gives me the thumbs-up for understanding him at last.